A BIG HIT
IN PELICAN BAY

By
L.C. Goldman

L.C. Goldman

Publishing

airleaf.com

ACKNOWLEDGMENTS

Dedicated to the memory of my wife Roslyn who passed away recently. Her inspiration, love and unconditional support made writing this novel possible.

People who live by a bay or on a bay relish enjoying the beauty of nature in all its glorious comings and goings. Living life enhanced by blazing, dazzling, multi-colored sunrises and spell-binding spectacular sunsets. Especially the sunsets, once romanticized by a song many moons ago called Moonlight Bay.

Florida is a state where the sunrises and sunsets rise and fall over a vast number of bays. Some famous, some infamous it seems. In Tampa, Florida, their bay is famous for the Tampa Bay Buccaneers, a professional football team. Every Sunday, from September to December, legal mayhem is committed and permitted when big bad Bucs butt heads and make violent contact with equally big-bodied men on teams like the land-locked Green Bay Packers or the San Francisco Forty-Niners, from that wonderful city by the bay.

Infamous, however, since they collide on a field like gladiators of yore, before thousands of blood-thirsty spectators, with the intent to inflict bodily harm on their adversaries. And yet not one of these big "bad" men is ever brought before the bar of justice for criminal behavior.

Near Miami Beach, Florida is the beautiful, serene Biscayne Bay, playground of many rich and famous. Where an infamous President cavorted in the sand with a somewhat shady character named after the pellets shot out of a B.B. gun. This President later committed political suicide covering up a third-rate burglary in a place called Watergate, but was never brought before the bar of justice. The bar of public opinion brought about his resignation.

In the '70's, in a sleepy little town tucked away in the southwest quadrant of Florida was over 2500 acres replete with mango preserves, wetlands, trees with nesting habitats for a varied species of birds, white sandy, virgin-like beaches uninhabited by humans, but living quarters for eggs deposited by turtles. And the calm, multi-colored waters of the Gulf of Mexico.

This sleepy town just south of this untouched area was called Naples. It had its own bay...Naples Bay. Hardly known for anything but little fishing boats that found their way to the Gulf of Mexico for excellent fishing. Crime was rarely a problem.

In the mid '70's a drastic change took place. Westinghouse developed the 2500 acres and created another bay, albeit a land bay. This soon to be upscale residential community was aptly named for the abundance of Pelicans who fished in the Gulf of Mexico. It was called Pelican Bay.

Seventy odd communities were built around a championship golf course and in only twenty five years became one of the most affluent places in the United States. It attracted, and became the private enclave for people with impressive business and professional credentials who wanted peace and quiet; the sun, sand, surf, flora and fauna, as well as the spectacular sunrises and sunsets. Once again crime was something that barely existed.

However, the serenity and peaceful existence was about to change. Crime would rear its ugly head. In the year 2005, unknown to most of the almost 10,000 residents of Pelican Bay, a vicious mob hit was being planned. Two of the many faceless people living that private, unfettered life were planning to murder a fellow resident.

Patrick and Bridget Halloran, husband and wife for over twenty years, using assumed names of Tully and Elaine Sullivan resided in the appropriately named community called The Sanctuary.

They were hiding out there in safe seclusion from their checkered pasts as one of the first man woman assassin teams working for the Masucci mob family in the Chicago area. Sullivan was only one of the many aliases this deadly duo used in their "hits-for pay" work over the past ten years.

Naples and their Pelican Bay sanctuary was not a random choice. Their target was a former soldier in the mob, now on the Witness Protection Program. He was a key witness who testified in the first trial of Don Mario Masucci. And was being stashed away to possibly testify if there was a second trial.

However, his new name was unknown. Residence unknown. New face unknown except to the plastic surgeon. All information known to the mob placed him living in Pelican Bay.

Finding their prey and executing the job was the part they enjoyed thoroughly. Pathological thorougness. Barely surpassed for their love of the

One Million Dollars that Masucci would be paying them for the hit.

Since they literally had time to kill, they decided to enjoy living the good life even as they planned wasting the life of someone they neither knew or cared to know.

The Sullivans belied their sinister way of life. They were quite ordinary people with an extraordinary occupation. Self-employed and commanding large sums of money for their work. They looked ordinary. Dressed ordinary. Acted ordinary. A low profile was their modus operandi.

This enabled them to melt into the retirement lifestyle of the residents of Pelican Bay. They partook of the many activities that the Bay offered and was renowned for. They played doubles tennis almost daily, but rarely with the same opponents. Making friends was not on their social agenda. It wasn't that they were unpleasant or rude, but unwilling to allow any person or persons to get close. They spent their 45 minutes on the court and left.

No hellos and no goodbyes. People viewed them as the odd couple.

They rode bicycles or walked a few miles every other day. They used the beach to full advantage. Every day about 11:30AM they would have the beach attendant set up two lounges and an umbrella in an isolated part of the beach. Well removed from other beach goers. They swam, they read and if someone from their tennis group said hello, they just nodded. The odd couple acting odd.

They had lunch at a corner table for two at the beach restaurant, The Sandpiper. The hostess knew them by name, but they barely acknowledged she was there. They ordered lunch, but never said one word to the waitress except to order.

Anonymity was not difficult in the heart of Pelican Bay. Although it was a haven for retired and semi-retired captains of industry and other professional men and women, people gave other people space. If one wanted to travel the path alone, no one volunteered to join.

There was a quiet aura at Pelican Bay, although in season almost 10,000 people were in residence in the condominiums, villas, town houses, single-family homes and in the towering high-rise buildings adjoining the beach and overlooking the Gulf of Mexico.

There rarely was an outpouring of people meandering on the tree-lined boulevard that ran down Pelican Bay from South to North for about three miles. An occasional jogger or dog walker or bicyclist. Workers pruning bushes and mowing the median grass. An occasional police car on the lookout for speeders exceeding the 30MPH limit.

It's almost as if thousands of residents were surreptitiously helicoptered in at some late hour, never to be seen again.

Not so for Tully and Elaine Sullivan. They made the extreme effort to be inconspicuously conspicuous among the many people who shared their passion for tennis; spending lazy mornings at the beach; visiting the library to soak up as much information as they could about Pelican Bay; having lunch at the beach restaurant or dinner at one of the toney restaurants on beautiful Fifth Avenue South.

They looked and acted like any other retired couple enjoying their golden years. One difference; their routine never varied. They did the same thing at the same time every day. Dinner time they were seen and known by name by the maitre'd's at Pazzos on Tuesday, Corks on Thursday and Zoe's on Saturday. 6:30 PM sharp in or out of season. This steady patronage guaranteed them a reservation in a secluded corner. A big tip didn't hurt.

However, many of their evenings were spent unlike other retirees. In their luxuriously furnished two-bedroom condo at the Sanctuary these cold-blooded killers were hard at work working out strategies and scenarios for the demise of the mob informer they were contracted to send to an early grave for $1,000,000.

It was never a question as to why that particular victim, but where, when and how. They were professional killers with time to kill and taking the time to painstakingly plan each detail to split-second perfection. Their reputation in the mob world as meticulous, thorough and 100% effective killers was legend. They never made a mistake, never left a clue. They had the Chicago police running around in circles as to their identity. That's why the cold case files on their five previous hits were still open. And totally frustrating to law enforcement.

Working on their killing plan was a business of pleasure and could have been worked on in any venue. It became infinitely more pleasurable when they learned that their quarry was living in Pelican Bay. It made living in this paradise that much more enjoyable.

So enjoyable that they decided that once the "job" was completed they would reward themselves by making Pelican Bay their permanent residence. They had the money from their previous hits, and the $1,000,000 would be the icing on the cake.

As usual, they talked about their target in abstract terms. Never, ever allowing conscience, remorse or any feeling of compassion to get in the way of the job at hand.

Yes, it was someone they knew about, but did not know personally. All they had to know was that the Don wanted him dead. The reason was of no importance. And never spent one single moment of their precious planning time thinking about that. The why was unimportant. Who was the only thing that mattered.

Search and destroy was their mantra. Get it done with dispatch. Get it done without leaving a single clue for police. Just find Salvatore Balviano, whatever his new name, whatever his disguise. Find out where he was holed up. And find the right moment to take him out. Then make sure Don Masucci sent the $1 million bucks post haste.

They realized that this "assignment" would be somewhat different then their previous hits for the Don. They never had to be concerned with someone on the Witness Protection Program. Local cops were one thing. The Feds were another.

Their plan: Make the rounds of everything going on in Pelican Bay. Visit the various places, take in all the events, check out the restaurants in the hope they would spot a swarthy, greasy-looking, muscle-bound mobster trying to pass as an ordinary retiree.

They were certain that no matter the new name or facial disguise, a mobster was still a mobster. No way of disguising that. That sooner or later he would revert to type and reveal his true identity.

They spent many evenings at Pelican Bay's pride and joy: The Naples Philharmonic. A magnificent structure that was the cultural center of Pelican Bay.

They enjoyed performances of well-known recording stars, comedians, major international artists, the best of the world's symphonic orchestras,

Broadway dramas and musicals, operas, ballet, jazz, pops and celebrated virtuosos like Itzhak Perlman.

Although they loved the elegance of the Phil and the diverse entertainment, they never lost sight for one moment why they were there. It enabled them to indelibly etch a mental picture of the hall just in case they spotted their target and had a chance to take him out on the spot.

They never sat in the same seats twice. They moved around the vast auditorium, in the orchestra or box seats, checking exits, usher deployment and police or other security. They envisioned a hit with 1500 people looking, but seeing nothing. The perfect distracted audience for that kind of blindness. And the perfect cover of bodies to provide an escape without being detected. Even though being inconspicuous was part of their plan, being overtly conspicuous was the other side of the coin. But not as the Sullivans.

It was a cleverly designed plan to create a smokescreen to mask their real identities and lead law enforcement officials down a garden path that would be a dead end. They had used this same M.O. in their previous hits, obviously with great success.

From time to time they would spend a weekend at either the famous Ritz Carlton, an elegant 5-star hotel that enchored the North end of Pelican Bay or The Registry hotel at the South end.

They would register under different names and pay in cash. The purpose was to establish an identity in each place of two oddball tourists who were spending a fun-loving weekend.

They changed appearances as well. Never looking the same. Outlandish disguises. Tully with a dyed brown toupee, a streak of blond in front, and sporting a full British-type brush mustache. He would also speak with a very broad Irish brogue.

Elaine was coifed in an outlandish red wig, garish makeup with deep red lips, long eyelashes and sun glasses with rhinestones worn in the darkish confines of the bar. She too, would speak with the thickest Irish brogue.

They spoke rather loudly and at times arguing over the silliest of things. And spent a great deal of time belting down Irish whiskey. Obviously being very obvious. Hoping to draw undue attention to their disguised personnas, while creating a public awareness of strange looking characters hanging around a bar. If and when the police would be searching for outsiders being in the area when the murder took place, they would be good candidates as suspects.

They took fiendish pleasure cavorting in their off-the-wall identities. However, these playful interludes contrasted sharply with the cold, calculating killers hidden under those disguises.

Detective Bill Sargent was seated at his desk in a little cubby hole in a rundown police precinct on the south side of Chicago. A desk with a lamp that barely gave any light. A cubby hole that was a poor excuse for an office. No windows, No doors. No plants. No pictures on the walls. No walls! Just gray partitions with patches of sweat where Sargent's head leaned against. Rap sheets and APB flyers of the ten most wanted were randomly strewn all around.

His feet were perched on the desk and his arms folded over his head. To anyone walking by he seemed to be napping. Only the ever present unlit cigar twirling around in his mouth gave him away. He stopped smoking ten years ago, but couldn't give up the idea of needing something to chew on: the addictive taste of tobacco.

In reality his mind was wide awake and spinning at 100 MPH about two issues in his life that were in constant conflict. He had turned in his retirement papers two days prior and debated the wisdom of such a move. Cop work was all he knew for the past twenty five years. He loved being a cop. The badge. The gun. The power. Taking down the bad guys.

On the other hand, retirement sounded like nirvana. No more perps, no stakeouts eating diet-busting donuts and drinking hot, stale coffee on cold, long nights. No busting into apartments expecting to be blown away by some maniac hot to kill a cop. Or chasing some twenty year old and finding his lungs bursting, his legs giving out after fifty yards.

But there was a catch. A real dilemma. What would he do with the days and particularly the nights of retirement? Mary was in the ground a year, and the wonderful things they planned to do over the next twenty five years were now a thing of the past.

All that aside, the real issue was his next assigned case. His last case. The Captain had briefed him and told him to follow up on an informants tip that the infamous Masucci mob had put out a contract on somebody, some place hiding out in the south. Not in South Chicago.

Following up on a Masucci hit tip was an unenviable 24 hour, every day, every week job. An exercise in futility more times than not. Simply because every day some stoolie would volunteer info, for a fee of course, about a contract on somebody, someplace in South Chicago or other points south.

All this did was have the cops scrambling around, chasing their tails. Very few, if any, ever panned out.

The Captain sarcastically said this tip was different. It involved the notorious man and woman hit team. A duo that Sargent had been fruitlessly chasing for over five years. They were suspects responsible for five contract hits of rival mob figures. Fruitless because there were never any forensic clues at the crime scene. No witnesses. The only tangible clue was tenuous at best. Informant after informant said that they were a man and woman that worked as a team. Contract killers with no ties to any mob family. No physical description. No names.

No ages. Not even a hint whether they worked out of Chicago. No other Chicago precinct had any information. Nothing from the FBI's mob group. Although the inside word was that they knew something about the hit team and their target, but cooperation with local authorities was not forthcoming. The Bureau had its own agenda when it came to mob activities and they weren't about to share that information.

Sargent knew he would be chasing ghosts. Just the thing his vindictive Captain relished. He disliked Sargent with a passion and would always give him the worst assignments.

However, there seemed to be one tangible lead that came from a C.I. inside Masucci's headquarters. The hit would take place in the south. Not the south side of Chicago, but the southern part of Florida.

Why South Florida? Who knows? Barely a tangible lead. Not even reliable from the mouth of the informant. Just a sense of what the mole in the hole heard in various conversations that there would be a hit, and maybe in Florida.

The tip notwithstanding, Sargent was hoping that the cold case files on the five murders, that had never really warmed up, would be assigned to another detective in his precinct. Or even another precinct.

He was fed up with being singled out by his vengeful Captain to bust his ass on cold cases, and nothing to go on. Just spinning his wheels.

Maybe this time would be different, since he had time on his side. His papers were in, and retirement was soon to enjoy. As bleak as that prospect might be.

When the Captain called him into his office, he was certain retirement was just a drink away until he called him Sarge. This was the Captain at his sarcastic best. He knew the Captain was mocking him and about to drop a bombshell.

Sargent hated to be called Sarge and the Captain knew it. Every uniform cop in the precinct taunted him by calling him Sarge. This was never a joke to the Sergeants of the uniform cops. They resented an over-the-hill detective being called Sarge. A perceived insult to the rank of Sergeant.

There was no beating around the bush. The order was simple and direct. Pick up the case files on the five old murders, brief himself on the details, talk to the M.E. about any forensic evidence, and then take the first plane leaving for Orlando, Florida. The police there work with an informant who has some information about the hit team and where the hit might take place.

"What evidence"?

"Whatever."

When Sargent asked about his retirement papers status, the Captain sarcastically said he would have

14

the rest of his life to lie on the beach or drink himself to death...after the case was solved.

"Solved, he blurted out, it's been years and we don't have a clue."

"You have one now, SARGE. Get with it. And don't give me any more lip."

Sargent realized it was futile to continue the discussion. He knew the score. Resign and jeopardize his pension or take the assignment and let futility be his companion for a long time.

The Captain had it in for him and what better way to keep his non-retiring detectives happy, and in line, then to give good old Sarge a case that would keep him out of his sight, yet under his thumb for weeks. Months. Maybe a year.

His papers were sitting on the Captain's desk, so with his new orders he was still a cop. Someone the Captain could use as a patsy without causing a mutiny in his department. Sargent was not only disgruntled but livid, but knew there was no higher authority out there to appeal his case. The son-of-a bitch knew exactly how to get his pound of flesh by giving him an impossible assignment that had stumped the entire Chicago police department for years.

He turned quickly, shrugged his shoulders and left the Captain's office. He managed to smile when a positive thought popped into his mind.

"Look at the bright side, he mumbled to himself. If I crack the case. I go out as a hero cop. Awards and all. An embarrassment to the Captain and all the naysayers. Besides what else do I have to do. Retirement sounded good if I said it fast, but probably was a death sentence. Or a life of boredom at best."

"I'll stay alive, Captain Bligh. Watch my steam. I'll make you regret ever turning me loose."

Pelican Bay was not only a Garden of Eden, a paradise for its residents, with almost perfect weather all year round, but an environmentalists dream. Acres of Mangrove preserves, never to be developed, ringed the area. White sandy beaches in stark contrast to the multi-colored water of the Gulf of Mexico. Beaches that became havens for Loggerhead Turtles who rose out of the Gulf to lay their eggs on those pristine beaches. Birds of all kinds flitting and darting along the many canals. Wood Storks nesting in private accommodations in the trees. An occasional alligator basking in the sun.

For those interested in cultural pursuits, Pelican Bay had that in spades. The beautiful Philharmonic that featured performers of all theatrical diversity. The very imposing new Museum of Art, displaying a beautiful permanent collection, as well as featuring retrospectives of famous artists, old and new, sculptors and photographers from all four corners of the world

A new 25,000 square foot community center soon to open with a huge fitness center.

Social activities abounded. Tennis, golf, think tank groups, men's discussion forums, year-rounder soirees, a thousand member women's league. Shopping at the elegant Waterside complex. Residents participated in self-government: The Foundation Board; The Pelican Bay Property Owners Association whose function was to keep dues paying members apprised of what the Foundation Board was doing. To be the omsbudman guarding the interests of their members.

MSTBU, an advisory board of Pelican Bay residents, appointed by Collier County Commissioners to oversee beautification projects, storm water management, street lights, signage, median landscaping, mangrove restoration, establishing a yearly budget and maintaining a high level of security by budgeting a great deal of money to utilize the services of The Sheriff's Department on a 24/7 basis.

This last item was of great interest to the Sullivans. They attended meetings to get a first hand reading of the pattern of police activity. How often they patrolled the area; the times of day; how many officers and cars; how quickly they responded to emergency calls. And most important what kind of security there was at The Naples Philharmonic, before, during and after performances.

Elaine joined The Women's League. Tully attended meetings of The Foundation Board, The

Property Owners and the MSTBU. They were seen but not heard.

They literally soaked up the myriad of problems being discussed as easily as they soaked up the rays of sun at the beach.

They always kept an eye out for the one person who might be their hit. Reasoning that somehow, someway they would find him. It was a long shot, they knew, but they were good at stuff like that. Maybe they would hit the mother lode before getting more information from Masucci.

With summer season in full swing and 80% of the Bay residents back in their northern homes, the Sullivans decided to take a brief vacation. They would spend a weekend where the people from the north came south, kids in hand, to enjoy the wonders of Disney World and Epcot Center in Orlando.

They flew there and arrived at almost the exact time as Detective Bill Sargent.

As if fate was pulling the strings, or there was an unexplained alignment of the planets, they all walked side by side to the baggage claim section. And then to the taxi stand.

The line for cabs was long and when the Sullivan's number came up the dispatcher asked what hotel they were going to. When they said the Marriot, he asked if they would mind sharing the cab with the next single passenger going to the same hotel.

Bill Sargent thanked them profusely and sat next to Elaine Sullivan. For the first few minutes there was no conversation, until Sargent apologized for not introducing himself. They reluctantly acknowledged and mumbled their names. When Sargent said he was from Chicago, they loosened up and said so were they. The conversation quickly became quite animated with each mentioning a favorite restaurant, local places of interest and a passionate interest in a favorite Chicago professional team. The Sullivans loved the White Sox and hated the Cubs. Sargent vice-versa. The Bulls were on everyone's radar. Mostly because of Michael Jordan. They both were ecstatic about "Da Bears", The Chicago Bears. More so when Mike Ditka was coaching.

However, when the conversation got around to career, the conversation came to a screeching halt when Sargent said he was a cop, a detective on assignment. Not another word was spoken until the Sullivans said goodbye leaving the cab. Sargent was taken aback by their obvious coolness, downright icy cold behavior after their friendly, "you know, I know, I like, you like" conversation, when he said he was a cop.

Maybe that turned them off, he thought. Scared them a bit. People are sometimes scared by cops. Or maybe still they had something to hide from the cop. Strange though. He made a mental note to check them out when he got back to Chicago, if they had any priors.

No matter. Time was of the essence and couldn't waste it trying to figure out why people did what they did.

His appointment with the Orlando police chief, and the face to face with the informant was two hours off. Barely enough time to prepare a list of questions for both.

When he got to his room he unpacked his one bag and threw things in one of the drawers. Not neatly. Socks on top of underwear, shirts mixed in with stained ties. The pants and jacket he was wearing needed pressing, but that would have to wait. Although his pants and jacket always needed pressing.

The exact opposite took place with his personal items. He meticulously placed his toiletries on the bathroom vanity ledge. He was compulsive about these items being in order. The toothbrush next to the toothpaste, closest to the sink. The razor next to the shaving cream. The comb next to the brush. Listerine last in line.

He smiled when he thought about his quirkiness. Clothes shoved in a drawer haphazardly, but his toiletries lined up like soldiers standing guard. When did that goofiness begin, he wondered? Mary always felt that his Mother must have pounded bathroom habits into his head at a very early age.

After washing up and washing out his mouth with Listerine, he sat down on the bed and wrote out a list of questions for the Chief, and particularly for the informant.

Some were benign questions, sort of his own polygraph exam to establish a true or false base. Others to confirm or validate the info given. Twenty plus years of interrogating low-life criminals and those Machiavellian minds gave him an insight whether the info was credible. When he finished he still had over an hour before the meeting.

He took out the cold case files and read them for the tenth time, hoping against hope that some little clue he missed before would pop out and really link up the five murders, or target who the killers were.

For the tenth time one little detail stood out. And was noted in each of the files. All the people interviewed when the homicide detectives canvassed the area made mention of a couple hanging around who spoke with a broad Irish brogue.

No detective working on any of the cases ever reported looking for such a couple to reinterview them. Why wasn't it ever highlighted as a significant clue? Curious, thought Sargent. Incompetent police work? Laziness? And they thought he was worn out and washed up, much less couldn't think straight because of the booze factor. Don't sell Bill Sargent short he mumbled to no one in particular.

He added to his list of questions to ask about Irish accents. Maybe the informant knew of hit men that were Irish. He looked at his watch and realized he had about a half hour. I'll get there a little early, he thought. He used a towel to shine his shoes to just plain dirty and left. He knew he was on a fool's journey, but that's what cop work was all about.

As he closed the door, he realized the growling he heard in the hall was his stomach telling him it needed some fuel to keep him going. In rushing from Chicago to the airport, he missed having breakfast. He stopped at the coffee shop in the lobby and ordered his usual: tuna on rye, no lettuce, light on the mayo and tea with milk. Make sure to include two pickle pieces.

When he looked up he saw the Sullivans at the end of the counter, facing opposite him. He waved, but they ignored him. They got up, paid their check and left abruptly. Bill Sargent smiled to himself about the obvious snub. He knew darn well they saw him because he saw the Sullivan woman poke her husband in the ribs and whisper something to him.

Sargent just shrugged his shoulders, took a sip of tea and ran over in his mind the check list of questions for the informant.

The Sullivans checked out of the hotel, a day in advance, and caught the next plane back to Naples.

Sargent got to the Police Station right on time and was ushered into the Chief's office. The informant, a dirty-looking, un-shaven, tall, skinny man wearing a ski cap, was sitting on the couch smoking a huge, smelly cigar.

Cheap as Sargent knew it was, the swirling, pungent smoke worked its way into his nostrils evoking a longing he thought was something in the past.

The Chief introduced Sargent to Fat Shorty, an oxymoron description if he ever heard one. Before he could ask one question on his long list, Fat Shorty blurted out in high, squeaky voice," The hit is on for next month. Don't know his name, but he's mobbed up. The Feds have him on the Witness Protection Program, holed up in Naples, at some rich place called Pelican Bay."

"Who's doing the hit", asked Sargent?

"Some guy and a broad. The same two that whacked the other five in Chicago. It's a Don Masucci contract to keep the guy from testifying in a trial. The word is there's one million clams to be paid."

How do you know all this," Sargent asked?

There was no response from Fat Shorty. Sargent pushed for more, but Fat Shorty stood up and backed toward the door. The Chief broke in and told Sargent that was all he would get.

"Fat Shorty is reliable, Detective. Everything he's given us in the past has panned out. If he had more to say he'd say it. The man's not bashful. He says his piece quickly and moves on."

"Too quickly, Chief. It's very sketchy with lotsa holes. The puzzle has some important pieces missing."

"It's a start, Sargent. At least you know where to look."

While they were talking, Fat Shorty walked out the door. No goodbye. No happy hunting. No nothing. The only thing he left behind was a trail of smoke.

"Naples, Chief? Where the hell is Naples? I gotta figure it's in Florida, right? Although with that Fat Shorty character it could mean Italy."

"And Pelican Bay! That sounds like a bird sanctuary, not where a big time mob hit will take place."

"Yeah, Florida. Way down in the Southwest corner of the state on the Gulf of Mexico. Don't know too much about Pelican Bay, but I hear it's a very rich community there."

"No matter what you think, detective, I would take Fat Shorty seriously. If he says it's going to happen there, it's going to happen there. I'd take book on it."

"Do you have a contact in Naples, Chief?"

"Sure do, a friend Sheriff Don Hunter. A good cop. Savvy and tough. Runs a tight ship. Knows his area well and what's going on. If anyone knows about a mobster hanging out there, he's your man."

"Do you want me to tell him you're coming?"

"Why? Do I have to?"

"He might be more cooperative if you come into town with an intro by a fellow cop. These southern sheriffs don't take kindly to a cop busting into his territory unannounced, especially from the big city."

"Appreciate that, Chief"

"Fat Shorty! Do you believe anyone who looks like that is believable?"

"Don't let his looks deceive you. He walks among the shadows of the mob scene and has an uncanny feel for what's going on. We trust him. What's more the mob trusts. So he gets around."

"Fat Shorty! And I thought Chitown had it's weirdos."

"Thanks for your time and help, Chief."

The Sullivans returned to The Sanctuary, showered and dressed for their usual 6:30 PM dinner at Pazzos. On the drive down 41 South to the restaurant not a word was spoken. They both had apprehensive looks on their face, but held their tongues. When Tully parked the car behind the restaurant, he unbuckled his seat belt and turned to Elaine and almost shouted," What do you think that cop was doing in Orlando?"

"Oh, I wouldn't read anything unusual into it Tully. Probably on a case where they had a lead on a someone suspected to be in the area."

"Uh, uh, naive wife", said Tully, vehemently shaking his head.

"He's looking for us. Somehow, someway he was directed to look for us in Orlando."

"Now, now, dear husband, that's a bit of paranoia. We've been in Naples all along and just by chance decided to go to Orlando. He doesn't have a clue that he's looking for for us. How could he ever know that we would be there."

"I know, I know. It's a stretch, my love, but we can never be too careful or too complacent. There's too much at stake. Our staying out of prison for one, and $1,000,000 if you haven't forgotten. All cops aren't stupid. Maybe they sent this Sargent guy because he's the bright one."

"Maybe he's bright, but he doesn't have a crystal ball."

"Oh well, for now I'll call it paranoia. Let's go. I could use a stiff drink, and a bowl of that great Tuscan bean soup. Lead on wife."

"That's more like it husband. That cop probably never heard of Naples, much less have any reason to suspect us."

Sargent returned to his room, showered and shaved and sent his suit out to be pressed. He wondered how much they would charge for one hour service.

He called the desk and asked the clerk about airline reservations to Naples, or how long it would take to drive. Three to four hours wasn't too bad and in any case would need a car in Naples.

He then called Sheriff Hunter and made an appointment for the next morning.

Sargent arrived in Naples a little after 6:00 PM and checked into the Inn at Pelican Bay, just a short distance from the North Naples Police Station where he would meet with Sheriff Hunter.

While registering he jokingly asked the clerk if Naples had a good restaurant with prices matching a very big expense account. And just the idea of being in a place called Naples whetted his appetite for a good Italian dinner.

"Ordinary Italian or the real stuff," asked the clerk.?

"Italian Italian."

"Pazzos on Fifth Avenue South is just that, Mr. Sargent. They're famous for their Tuscan menu."

"Love it. Make a reservation for one at 7:30 PM and please write down directions how to get there."

With the ever-present unlit cigar dangling from his lips, he gave the clerk his credit card and was promptly told the entire inn was a non-smoking building.

"Oh, I don't light up. Just chew on it a little bit to remind me that the lousy habit I had for years is now a thing of the past. It serves a purpose, though. Sort of a pacifier. Calms me down, and I seem to think better with it. I think."

"What time does the bar open in the morning? And how late does it stay open at night?"

"Just kidding."

Once settled in the room, he called the Captain and told him about Fat Shorty. That he was in Naples and could be reached at The Inn of Pelican Bay.

"Naples? Where's that? Never mind. Enjoy the weather, but not too much. You have a job to do."

"Speaking of jobs, Captain, what's with my retirement papers, sir"?

"Working on it Sarge. It's going as slow as I can make it go. Do your job. Retirement happens when the job is done. Got it Sargent?"

"Got it Captain. Coming through loud and clear. But that won't stop me from asking about it every time we speak."

"That's insubordination, Detective Sargent."

"What'll you do, Captain, sir, fire me?"

The phone went dead on the other end. That son-of-a-bitch, thought Sargent. Wish I had the balls to hang up first.

He got to Pazzos a little before 7:30. The very attractive hostess, with a body to die for, escorted him to a table in the corner near the bar. A very active bar with the young and beautiful people holding court. The noise was of mach 2 level.

"Just great," he mumbled out loud. "I won't be able to hear myself think. The food better be good for the beating my ears will take."

The Sullivans sitting at the opposite side of the restaurant saw Sargent being seated.

Tully looked at Elaine and quietly murmured, "my paranoia is not so paranoid after all. Right. He's here Elaine. Looking for us. Let's leave before he sees us."

"Cool it Tully. It's just a coincidence. He's not looking for us. It's a one-in-a-million coincidence. He may be looking for us, but I'm sure he doesn't know who us is."

"In any case if we leave now we only draw his attention. And get him thinking. Just sit tight. Eat your soup. Act nonchalant. Maybe he won't see us or even recognize us."

"Sure he'll recognize us. I want to know what the hell is he doing in Naples? He must have followed us here. It's no coincidence. Someone in Chicago must have tipped him off to look for us here."

"Now who could that be Tully? Only the Don knows we're here and he ain't telling anyone. Much less the cops. It's only a coincidence I tell you. Pure and simple."

"Coincidence, dear wife? Sure. Meeting at the airport. Riding in the same cab. Staying at the same hotel in Orlando. Learning that we're from Chicago. Eating breakfast in the coffee shop with him peeking out over the menu at us. Waving like he's seen an old friend. Or somebody he's tracking down."

"That my dear, naive wife is not coincidence. That smacks of a clever homicide cop zeroing in on his prey. Stalking. Licking his chops, waiting to make the collar."

"Elaine, I think we should do what we do best. Take him out. The huntees should become the hunters. When he leaves here we follow and put the badge out of commission. Permanently."

"Not very smart, Tully. First of all I think we really are being paranoid. Secondly, we don't want to have the locals and Chicago police investigating the murder of one of their own. This place would be crawling with cops."

"My, my Elaine when did you take a course in psychiatry? Coincidence? Paranoia? What's next, crystal ball readings?"

"Shut up, Tully. Eat your soup. Have another drink and leave the thinking to me. That's what we've always done and it's worked perfectly. There's no damn good reason to change now."

"I know exactly what to do. We'll follow him alright, but just to find out where he's staying. Then I'll find a way to accidentally on purpose bump into Detective Sargent. I'll bat my eyelashes and wiggle my ass and find out what he knows or doesn't know."

"What I do know is that he would have done something in Orlando if he had a clue that we're the guys he's looking for. If, in fact he's even looking for us."

"Okay, Mama knows best, but watch your wiggling backside. Remember, he's a gold badge Chicago detective, not some local hick cop that spends his time ticketing drivers who honk their horns, catching snowbirds that don't fully stop at full stop signs."

They ate in silence, keeping one eye on Sargent. Ordered their waitress to prepare a check and waited til he paid his and left. They left moments later, following in their car at a distance, fully aware that an experienced detective might have a sixth sense that he was being tailed.

When he pulled into The Inn at Pelican Bay, Elaine shrieked with joy. "Now that is coincidence," she yelled at Tully.

"What the hell does that mean," he muttered?

"Tomorrow I'm going to a fashion show and if he's around I'll find a way to bump into the good detective."

"Don't be too obvious, smarty pants. A good detective always has his antenna up about accidently-on-purpose-run intos. Be careful."

"You worry too much, Tully. He's probably one of the many Chicago detectives that's been looking for us for years. He and anyone else in the Chicago P.D. doesn't have a clue who they're looking for. You know why? Because there aren't any clues. They're groping in the dark and there's no light anyplace."

"But just to satisfy any concerns you have, I'll get close to him and find out why he's here and what he knows or thinks he knows about who he's looking for. Even if I have to go to bed with him."

"What?"

"Thought that would get your full attention, Tully baby. Just kidding about the bed thing. Just kidding."

The next morning, Sargent met with Sheriff Hunter only to learn he had little or no information about any suspected hit team operating in the Naples area.

He did say that a friend of his in the State's Attorney's office in Tallahassee once mentioned that a person or persons in the Federal Witness Protection Program had been relocated in Florida. Possibly Naples and possibly in the Pelican Bay area. The rumor had been circulating for more then six months, but nothing concrete. No name. No specific address. No indication that one or more persons were being protected from the mob or were material witnesses in a high profile murder or racketeering case.

Sargent left the Sheriff's office convinced that there was a window of opportunity, although just a slight crack, that there was a witness being stashed away to keep him from a mob hit. And if here was in Naples, Pelican Bay, the hit team probably was here, too. Ready to take him out at some future time.

Nothing great to work on, but when he returned to the inn he made some calls to friends at his precinct and a very close friend at the FBI. Nobody knew anything about someone from the Chicago area with mob ties, who was on the WP list residing in Florida, much less Naples. They volunteered to check other jurisdictions in the Midwest and call if anything surfaced. However, he felt his FBI friend was not quite forthcoming. Something was there. But what?

Chewing on his ever present unlit cigar, Sargent felt buoyed by the Sheriff's tiny shred of unsubstantiated info. Rumors have a way of becoming reality in the police business. Besides that his twitching nose told him he was on the right track. Where the station was he didn't know. Fat Shorty had pointed him in the right direction. Maybe he did have inside info.

If nothing else, it was a start.

It was twelve noon straight up, and even though his bio clock was still on Chicago time, he felt the need for a drink to celebrate his tiny bit of good fortune. As sketchy as that was. But since when did he need good fortune to celebrate with a drink or two. Or three. More often than not it was lots of bad fortune that drove him to drink. And be drunk.

The bartender was friendly and apologized for all the women flitting around the bar. Disturbing the peace for all the serious male drinkers.

"There's a fashion show going on in the other room and the broads are drawn to that like a moth to a flame," he said softly. "They don't drink, but they sure smell good."

Sargent finished his second drink and got up to leave. As he turned he almost knocked down Elaine Sullivan.

"Detective? Aren't you Detective Sargent? I hope you remember me. My husband and I shared a cab with you on the way to the Marriot Hotel in Orlando."

"Yeah, right. You're that rabid White Sox fan, but forgive me for forgetting your name Mrs..."

"Sullivan. ELAINE Sullivan" Emphasizing Elaine.

"I apologize Mrs. Sullivan. I have a small problem. Always forget a name and barely remember a face. In your case it's the exception, the face is too pretty to forget so easily."

"I think that's a compliment, Detective."

"How's your husband?" Is he here with you?"

"Tully? No, he doesn't give up a tennis date for anything. Especially for a woman's thing. Tennis or golf that's what retired execs do when they live in paradise."

"What brings you to Naples, Detective? Or are you just vacationing in Florida, traveling from one sunny place to another?"

"Well the sunshine feels pretty good, Mrs. Sullivan, especially since it's 20° in Chicago according to a gloating weatherman on television here."

"But to answer your question more accurately, I'm sort of on a working vacation. Cleaning up a case with the Naples police and then tracking some people I haven't seen in years."

"Do they live in Pelican Bay? Are they friends from Chicago.?"

"I heard they live in some kind of a bay in Naples, and yes they're from Chicago. Haven't seen them in years. They don't expect me and I want to surprise them. I have a special gift for them, sort of payment for something way back when."

"What are their names? Maybe they're friends of ours. Tully and I are members of many organizations here and maybe we've met them at meetings or at parties."

"I appreciate that, Mrs. Sullivan, but that would sort of defeat my purpose. The surprise, that is. Thanks anyway."

"Sorry to be rude, but I have to run off now. Gotta see the Sheriff about tieing up some loose ends. Give my regards to Mr. Solomon."

"Sullivan, Tully Sullivan."

"Sorry about that ma'am. It's that name remembering defect. You've just made it easier, however. I'll just think of Tully Sully. That should do it, if I run into you two somewhere."

"Before you go Detective, why don't we turn that somewhere into sometime soon. For dinner or a drink. Our apartment or at a wonderful restaurant called Pazzos. The martinis are perfect and the food Italian Italian."

"That's very kind of you, Mrs. Sullivan, but I wouldn't want to impose on you and your husband, even if I had the time."

"I wasn't including my husband, Detective. He's usually busy most evenings with some kind of Pelican Bay board meeting. I thought it might be nice for two old windy city residents to continue our conversation about the Cubs and the White Sox. And maybe start a drive to get Ditka to come back and coach the Bears."

"Well, I don't know how long I'll be in Naples, Mrs. Sullivan. If I find my friends quickly, I'll be on my way."

"Call me Elaine, Detective. I hate formality. Why don't I call you tomorrow and hope you're still around. I assume you're staying at the Inn?"

"It seems a little awkward, but if you assure me that your husband won't get the wrong idea, try me."

"I doubt that Tully would get the wrong idea. We're both open-minded about our open marriage. He always wants me to enjoy myself while he does his executive thing."

"Tomorrow then, Detective? I'll pick you up around 7:00 PM."

"Call me just to be sure I'm here. By the way if I can call you Elaine, please call me Bill. Detective sounds too police-like."

"Bill it is. Have a good day and bring your appetite tomorrow."

Back in the room, Sargent called Harry Diner, one sergeant in his precinct that he could trust, and asked him to check out a Mr. and Mrs. Tully Sullivan, her name Elaine. About 55 to 60 years old. Chicago people.

"I'll hold Harry. Need the info ASAP."

"No such people on record, Bill. Checked the phone book, the DMV, outstanding warrants and voting registration. No nothing, anyplace. Are you sure that's their real names?"

"Not sure of anything. How far did you go back?"

"Ten years. The only Tully Sullivan around that age died three years ago."

"Thanks Harry. Do me a favor though and forget we ever talked."

"Sure thing, Bill. Why the secrecy? Aren't you working the case of that hit team who whacked those five goons.?"

"No secret, Sergeant. The less the Captain knows about any progress I'm making the better. Might get my retirement papers off his desk and into the right hands with a little giddyap."

"Tully, the cop took the bait. And I didn't even have to wiggle my ass. Just let him brush my boobs a bit. We're having dinner tomorrow at Pazzos."

"Without me?"

"Of course, without you. How can I put my femme fatale charm to work with you in the picture. That and a few glasses of good Chianti Reserva might loosen his lips a bit. I'll find out what he's really up to. That stuff about wanting to surprise some old friends is plain B.S. Can't believe he said it with a straight face."

"Good. Just remember Miss Femme Fatale that vino or those Cosmopolitans have an effect on you, too. Be sure it doesn't loosen your tongue. He's a cop, and anything you say he'll filter through that cop mentality."

They sat in a booth at the back of the restaurant. As the tables started to fill up, and the bar got its usual raucous crowd, the noise level made it difficult to hold a meaningful conversation. Elaine Sullivan moved as close to Bill Sargent without actually sitting in his lap. He felt uneasy as her low-cut dress, revealing her ample cleavage, was directly in his line of sight. He tried to focus on her eyes, but lost that sight battle.

He was amazed at how quickly she polished off a Cosmopolitan Martini, then a second one. Finishing that, she followed with a glass of a very good Chianti Reserva. Good thing he was on the Captain's charge account. She was almost finished with her glass of wine, while Sargent was still only half-way through his first glass. The more she drank, the closer she inched up to the already embarrassed Sargent. Meanwhile carrying on a one-sided conversation.

She was being very obvious, he thought to himself. "What did she want? Sex? No way. Information about what he was doing so far from Chicago? And why? Definitely."

Sargent knew that the sex was far from a remote possibility.

He may have been attractive a long time ago, but after twenty years of drinking and smoking and long nights on stakeouts his face was weather beaten, wrinkled, with a red, veiny nose.

Only Mary found him attractive. She never saw the warts, maybe because she drank as much as he did, smoked twice as many cigarettes and had that same debauched look. She adored his look. Loved that face. Sex wasn't very important. Twenty plus years of marriage was.

He didn't think sex was on Elaine Sullivan's mind either. As a street cop in Chicago even hookers didn't make passes at Bill Sargent. And as a detective, no female suspect thought to curry favor by crossing and uncrossing her legs when being questioned.

No sir, it wasn't sex. So what did this very attractive, stacked Elaine find so interesting in a face that looked like a clenched fist?

Was it his gun? He laughed to himself that he equated his gun with the thing hanging between his legs that hadn't fired in a long time.

When the waitress took their dinner order, Elaine ordered another bottle of wine.

"Whoa, I don't think my Detective's budget can afford another $50 bottle of Chianti Reserva."

"Oh, I'm sorry, Bill, I forgot to mention that everything is on me. The dinner and the wine are with the blessing of Tully Sullivan's Platinum American Express Card."

When he started to object, she placed two fingers on his lips, but never uttered a word. Her eyes spoke volumes.

Now he was absolutely certain that the lady had something else in mind, so he sat back and for the first time relaxed. The second glass of wine really was relaxing. He waited for Sullivan to reveal her real reason for this expensive dinner.

For more than a half hour, nothing. Pleasant conversation. Uncomplicated. Non inquisitive. Revealing nothing. Just about the Cubs, The White Sox, The Bears and The Bulls. Sports seemed to be her passion and proved it by knowing more stats about players and teams that he barely touched on.

She talked, he listened. Something he did in all his investigative work. The more someone talked, the more someone might reveal something not normally would be revealable. Especially when alcohol was in the picture. The tongue got a little looser, without thinking of the consequences.

When she started to catch her breath and in the middle of spouting off Walter Payton's history-breaking rushing stats, Sargent interrupted for the first time.

"Elaine, where did you and Tully live in Chicago?"

With wide open eyes, she almost gasped, somewhat taken aback by the abruptness of the question.

"Well...er...we really didn't live in Chicago. I was born and raised In Milwaukee and Tully in Minneapolis. However since we were on the road, selling our line of cosmetics, Chicago was a port of call for three months or more each year. Sometimes consecutive months. We stayed at a downtown hotel and our selling right there. The same hotel for over seven years...so you might say we were second city residents when asked. Love Chicago and wish I could have called my birth city."

She hurried through this explanation virtually without taking a breath. And without missing a beat changed the subject.

"Do you travel often out of state looking for criminals?"

"Sometimes, not very often."

"Is this one of those sometimes or just plain old playtime?"

"I must confess, Elaine, I've not been totally truthful. I'm not in Florida for sun and fun. I'm working on some cold case murders, til my retirement papers go through. It's my Captain's way of punishing me for all my years of insubordination. He just hates my guts."

"Cold cases? Why did they warm up?"

"They didn't really. Just got a little tepid."

"What does that mean?"

"We had a series of unsolved hits on mob figures in the past five years and we were tipped off that there was a connection in Florida."

"My dear Captain felt this was good way to get me out of his hair and delay my retirement. Very vindictive."

"What kind of tip?"

"Not very substantial, but police work doesn't need something substantial. We go after the smallest lead because it might lead to a bigger. Even an arrest."

"In this one I'm looking for a man and woman with thick Irish brogues who may have seen something at each murder. There's no evidence that they were involved, but the fact they were at the scene each time seemed a little odd. Maybe just coincidence. Sometimes people have a morbid curiosity about murder. They are not suspects, but may have some information that would be helpful. We believe that a man and woman working as a team are the killers. Is there any link? Who knows?"

"That's the extent of the cases warming up. In my opinion I'm on a fools errand. And will probably toss in the towel soon and force the Captain to turn in my papers."

"Interesting, Mr. Detective. Tully and I are Irish through and through. Are we suspects?"

"Only if you had a thick Irish brogue and murdered five people."

"You certainly lead an exciting life, Bill. Sniffing around for clues. Tracking down killers. Wearing that gold badge and carrying a gun. What power."

"Far from it. Highly overrated. It's really just a rat race. A race where the rats rarely take the bait, and win out very often. Most of the time the work is boring and tedious."

"Boring, boring. Boringly routine. In this stage of my career and life, a cold case file is the ideal refuge for a cop that's on his way to a home. A home where old, unwanted cops reside. Or some bar where the bartender keeps the drinks coming without asking."

"Come on, Bill, that seems much too modest. I feel you are very good at what you do. Contrary to what your Captain thinks." "However, I know exactly what you mean. The business world is not too different. Other then the money, what we did was boring, too. Tully and I got out of our rat race because we found ourselves running after the bait."

"We always thought retiring was the end of the line. It was a refreshing change to come to paradise here and lead an unexciting life of retirement. Not the end, but the beginning of a new way of life. This is where we run around at a snail's pace. Where the sun shines every day; the climate and temperature almost perfect year 'round; the Gulf waters warm and gentle; and the martinis icy cold."

"That's sounds more like it, lady. That's my idea of retirement.   No killers. No cold case files. No despotic captain getting on my case all the time. No chasing ghosts. No guns."

"Just sitting at the end of a pier; fishing pole in hand, and not caring if the fish are biting. Better still sitting at the end of my favorite bar. Just sitting, thinking of nothing."

"Yes, in a few days, I'm gonna close up shop in paradise. I'll tell a little white lie to the Captain that there's nothing in Florida remotely connected with the hits in Chicago, and politely suggest he turn in my papers."

"What about finding your friends?"

"No luck there either. Maybe they went back to Chicago. In any case I'll get the first stage out of town and go to a Bears game when I get back. Then prepare to vanish into retirement as quickly as possible."

"And while on the subject of retirement, I think I'll fold up my napkin and retire for the night. It's been a long, tiring day. The foods been great. The company stimulating. But one more glass of wine and I might just confess to the murders myself."

"Oh! Don't leave. I thought the evening was just getting started? I had so many more things to discuss."

"I'm not only a Chicago sports nut, but cops intrigue me no end. I watch all the cop shows on TV, and since I have the ear of a real live one I'd love to hear more about those cold cases."

"Not much to add, Elaine. I know less then nothing about who the killers are, where they are and what they're doing right now. In truth I can't even make up things to hold your interest."

"Old Bill is just playing out the string, following orders, making my Captain believe my nose is to the grindstone. The only real stone I care about is the one not left unturned until my papers get through the system."

"If you must go...can we do this again before you leave?"

"Thanks for the invite, but no thanks. I'm not sure Mr. Sullivan would appreciate a cop seeing his wife for the second time. Besides, I'm somewhat uncomfortable having a lady pay for my food and drink."

"Elaine, let me return the favor and be a gentleman by walking you to your car. I want to be sure the bad guys don't try and take advantage of such an attractive lady."

"Don't bother, Detective. I'm quite capable of taking care of myself."

She managed a weak smile, mumbled good night and walked quickly out of the restaurant, never looking back.

Sargent started to follow, but got the message and walked slowly out the door, with a broad grin on his face. He felt certain that Elaine Sullivan knew something about the forthcoming hit. She is too smooth and slick, he thought. A bit too slick for her own good. He decided to stay in Naples for a while longer and poke around and see what else he could find about Mr. and Mrs. Tully Sullivan. Are they my Irish connection, he wondered?

"Early night, Elaine? The femme fatale's wiggling backside didn't get the dick to talk?"

"It worked Mr. wise-ass. Got him to talk plenty that he's looking for two people with thick Irish accents. Man and wife or just male and female. The Chicago cops have great interest in some cold cases. Guess what? Our previous hits back there. Sargent has the assignment."

"So I was right, he's looking for us."

"Half right. Yes, he's looking for us, but doesn't know who us is. Hopefully he'll stop at the Ritz Carlton and learn about the two very Irish people with broad accents who were at the bar recently. That should keep him busy for awhile."

"What else does he know?"

"Nothing. He doesn't have a clue. In fact he's throwing in the towel and leaving shortly to retire. He'll be out of our hair for good."

"Wrong Miss Charm Boat. I think he gave you just enough information that he's on to something. Just enough to have you let your guard down."

"Think about it, Elaine. Two people with Irish accents. That could mean Irish names. Man and wife or male and female. That's a bullseye on both accounts on us. An experienced cop doesn't divulge sensitive info like that in a restaurant to a virtual stranger. Does he suspect us, maybe not? But you can rest assure his antenna is up and his wheels are spinning in our direction. Five will get you ten he's burning up the wires to Chicago to get something, anything on the Sullivans."

"We can't afford to sit back and wait for him to walk in here and make a collar. We have to act as soon as we learn he hasn't left Naples in the next day or two. If he's still here, we have to assume Sargent's made us. And it's just a matter of time before he acts."

"Act? What the hell does that mean? Act what Tully?"

"Exactly what it means. Get him before he gets us."

"Well dear husband, you're acting like a birdbrain. If we take out Sargent then we draw undue attention to us in Naples. There'll be more Chicago dicks swarming all over than we can keep track of. Not to mention the locals. That might be the end of our act. The end of a million bucks."

"I think you're letting lots of imagination take over a limited intellect. We don't have any idea whether or not we're on his radar, or even will call Chicago."

"No doubt in my mind. He thinks we're from Chicago. Checking us out is routine with any cop. Doesn't that make sense?"

"Not if he doesn't think we're from Chicago."

"I thought he does?"

"Not after I told him we weren't. Just passed through on business from time to time."

"And he bought it?"

"Yeah, why not? Sargent has nothing on his mind except retirement. And God knows I tried."

"He's got the old cases because his boss doesn't like him and wants to give him grief about turning in his papers."

"Let him be, Tully. He's a worn-down, tired cop. Not a psychic."

"Okay, okay. We'll play it your way. For now. But my way is still in play if we find out that I'm right."

"Bill? Harry Diner. Got some info on that guy on the Witness Protection Program."

"Great, Harry."

"He's a former muscle guy for the Masucci family. Salvatore (Shrimpy) Balviano."

"Balviano? I busted him a few times for extortion and assault. What the hell did he do to be put on The WPP? Just a small-time hood. Not somebody important to get that kind of Fed protection."

"Yeah, a small-time goon, but for some reason he's considered a big-time witness by the Feds. The word is that he was on the inside of Masucci's operation, real close to the Don, and gave them enough information so that they could get an indictment against him. In return for immunity, he testified in a closed court hearing."

"The trial didn't go well for the government, even with Balviano, and Masucci got off. A hung jury."

"The Feds got word of threats against Balviano's life, so they put him on WPP and relocated him in Florida."

"Since they were going to retry Masucci, and Balviano would have to testify again, they gave him a face job, a new identity, and a new place to live."

"Masucci put out a contract on him, and the inside dope is that the Don gave his top hit team big bucks to take him out. It was his insurance policy if and when the canary would sing again in court."

"Any info about where in Florida, Harry?"

"South. That's all I know, Bill."

"Great stuff, Harry. Appreciate it. One other thing. What name is Balviano using now?"

"Can't get that. The Feds have put a steel curtain of silence around that piece of info. Only a handful of people know and they ain't talking. Under the penalty of death, I assume. The Feds want Masucci real bad and they're not taking any chances. Even Balviano's mother doesn't know his new name or where he's located. It's so tight that the Feds won't even admit that a Balviano exists."

"One small thing that might help in tracking him down. Balviano is a rabid opera lover. Can you imagine a mob muscle guy into opera? If there's an opera on tap where you are, check it out. You might find him on a line buying a ticket. With a little luck you could get to him before the hit team does."

"That's good to know, Harry, but I know a little secret about Shrimpy that not too many people are aware gives him away."

"What secret?"

"Now, Harry, my good friend, it wouldn't be a secret if I told you. Would it?"

"Don't you trust me?"

"Yep. You're one guy I trust, but a secret is a secret. That's why it's called a secret. I'll let you in on it when I find him, and more important the two who are out to get him."

"If Balviano leads me to them that's all that matters."

"Otherwise I couldn't less whether the canary is dead or alive."

"You know why I'm here. I want the two who killed those five. I spent many sleepless nights and a lot of blood and sweat working on those cases. And now that my dear Captain decided to put me back on this not so desireable assignment, I want them bad. Bad, my friend, so I can tell the Captain to stick this job where the light doesn't shine in his body. Retirement, Harry. That's all I want. And as soon as."

"Good hunting, Bill."

"You did great, Harry. I'll never forget you put your badge on the line for me. Never."

Sebastian Bach received the new season's brochure from The Philharmonic and turned to the section operas. Carmen, La Traviata and Tosca were all on the program for the coming season.

"Love that Carmen," he said out loud.

"Did you call me, Sebastian?"

"No Carmen. I was just thinking out loud about the opera Carmen coming to the Phil this season."

"Thinking is all you can do, Sebastian. The only Carmen in your life is me. You know the rules the Feds made very clear. Anything you did in your previous life is out"

"No opera. No Italian stogies. No Chianti. No pasta. Nothing Italian."

"No pasta, Carm!. That really hurts."

"Yeah, I know. And that goes for me, too."

"Remember, you're a Wasp from New Hampshire. If you want to live, that is."

"Oh, I know, Carm. Just wishing out loud. You can't blame me. It's tough to break old habits. However, I know the game. I'm a Lawrence Welk lover, a teetotaler, and a dues paying member of the anti-smoking league."

"Count on it."

"It's a good life here Sebastian. Let's live it as long as we can."

"At least for three months, Carm."

"What the hell do you mean?"

"I didn't tell, because I didn't want you to worry."

"Worry? I worry all the time. Tell me? Worry about what?"

"The Feds called and said I have would have to testify again. They're going to try Masucci again. Maybe three months."

"I got a bad feeling this time. Masucci will take me out. If not back in Chicago, then down here."

"The family doesn't give up on someone. They don't like rats. And the boss man will do anything, pay anything to keep me from putting him in the slammer."

"I wouldn't be surprised he gave the contract to those two who hit the five back when. They're good. The best. They never leave a clue. They appear out of nowhere and disappear into thin air."

"I wouldn't be surprised if they're down here to find me and put me in the ground. They never miss."

"Then let's beat them to the punch. Don't testify. Tell the Feds you refuse. Once was enough."

"Are you nuts? You don't cross the Feds. A deal is a deal. If I refuse to testify, they will drop me like a hot potato. No Witness Protection. No shield. No support money. And I wouldn't put it past them to get word to Masucci that we're here in Naples, in Pelican, under the name of Bach."

"Then we're two dead guineas."

"Let's not wait another day, Sebastian. We'll move."

"Move? Where the hell do we move to?"

"Maybe out of the country. South America. I hear Argentina is a good place. We have enough money. Most important we don't have an alternative."

"If you testify, this time Masucci will find a way to kill both of us. If we stay here the contract duo will finish us off. If we move we buy time. Maybe, just maybe, they never find us. Or after a while give up trying."

"Look Carmen, there's no alternative. First, the family never gives up when you've crossed them. Second, I don't trust the Feds to forget about us. If I weasel out of testifying they're are not above letting Masucci know we left the country. And they can find out where we go, even if it's the jungles of South America."

"So we'll fake going one place and go to another, Sebastian."

"Brilliant, Carm. Unless you forget, when we went to Sicily, you need a passport to leave the country. Who do you think can find out about anybody using a passport to skip town?"

"They can track us no matter how many times we try to fake them out by changing passports and changing destinations. And that goes double if we try to get fake passports."

"It's a bad idea. If we screw them they'll want our blood, and they'll make sure Masucci is the blood bank."

"Alright, maybe you're right. Stall them. Even refuse to testify when they want you, because that's sure death. Do something, anything to make it miserable for the Feds or Masucci to get a shot at you."

"Let me think about it, Carm. We still have some time. I don't know exactly what, but maybe we fake our own deaths."

"Meanwhile right now all this talk has given me an appetite. I'm starved. Get dressed and we'll go to Pazzos. Make a reservation."

"Bill? Elaine Sullivan. I'm glad you're still in town. Tully had to go to Miami on business for a few days, so I need some male companionship. Not to mention protection against all those bad guys out there. What better way then having a detective escort me to dinner. Meet me at Pazzos at 7:30. Please don't say no, because the reservation was made. And there's a penalty for cancelling. Ha. Ha."

"Not a good idea, Mrs. Sullivan."

"Elaine, remember?"

"Still not a good idea, whatever I call you. The Pazzo people know you by name and someone might slip up and tell Tully you were at dinner with a tall, dark, handsome Chicago detective."

"I really hope that's the case, Bill. He might get to show more interest in doing the mattress polka a little more often."

"Now you have me blushing, lady."

"If I accept your invitation, and I'm not saying I do, how about a change of venue. Someplace that fits my budget, really my Captain's budget, since it's my turn to flash plastic."

"Forget it detective. You have no turn. I asked you and I still have my trusty platinum card."

"It is nothing new. I've done this before when Tully went out of town, with his permission I might add. Besides the Pazzo people know to keep silent. Especially when I tip generously."

"Well if you insist. You just happened to catch me at a lonely, weak moment. Depressed a bit too, since my retirement papers still not have been retired."

"7:30 at Pazzos it is. I'll be wearing that tired look on my face and my only disheveled black suit with brown shoes. So you shouldn't have trouble picking me out."

"You may think you're turning me off, Mr. Cop, but I happen to like that look. I get enough of that suave, polished, GQ look at home."

Pazzo was crawling with people when Sargent arrived five minutes early. They were three deep at the bar, so the idea of getting a drink passed quickly.

At exactly 7:30 Elaine Sullivan sashayed in wearing a stunning Versace suit. The maitre'd greeted her with a hug and a kiss on both cheeks and escorted her to the usual booth in the corner.

Sargent was virtually ignored and tagged along, somewhat embarrassed by his disheveled appearance, right behind Mrs. Fashion Plate. And feeling terribly out of place. He sensed he was wearing a neon sign that said cop. Someone to be ignored. Or just tolerated since he was in the company of someone important.

A Cosmopolitan Martini appeared immediately for her "highness", and a glass of Chianti for the schlepp with her. The bottle not too far behind. He knew this was her game of sorts, to put a lowly cop at a social disadvantage. Sargent decided to play the game to the hilt. He raised his glass and with sarcasm dripping with every word remarked, "Elaine, I am privileged to be sitting at the table with an elite lady who commands this royal attention."

"Cute, Bill, very cute. Don't be defensive. I didn't do it to embarrass you. I just called in advance to be sure we didn't waste time waiting for our drinks. They're kind of slow many times, when it gets very crowded."

"I hope you're not offended?"

"To the contrary. I'm just amazed at the clout you have at this very classy restaurant."

"In Chicago, they know my name at the Greek diner. They serve my bacon and eggs the minute I park my backside on the stool. I consider that an honor. Your way is the better way. The way I knew the rich lived."

"Not as dramatic as you make it out to be, Detective. Rich is what they think, not what they know. And I get more out of what they think."

"Now that we're on the same level of recognition at our respective eating places, let's talk about something more tastefully interesting. Like what to order."

While they were looking at the menu, the dim light given off by the candle on the table was virtually reduced to no light by the imposing figure of the 6 foot, two inch, 210 lb Tully Sullivan.

"Mr. Sullivan," said a flustered Bill Sargent, as he knocked over a glass of water. "I...we...didn't"

"Yes, I know. You didn't expect to see me. Neither did my beautiful wife. Good evening Elaine. Enjoying yourself?"

"Tully? Miami, meetings, and driving, and back the same day? That's tiring love, isn't it?"

"Changed plans. Never went. Got all the information over the phone. Played tennis with Bob Stone instead. Had a late lunch and waited 'til dinner for you to get back. When you didn't show, I had the feeling you were out to dinner with a friend or other, so I called Pazzos, on a hunch, and lo and behold they said you'd be in at 7:30. Thought I'd surprise you cheating on me with another man. Only kidding about the cheating. More like enjoying yourself with another man."

"Isn't that one and the same, husband?. Don't answer and sit down and join us for a drink. I'm sure Detective Sargent wouldn't mind."

The glazed look on Sargent's face said it all. Not only was he surprised to see Tully Sullivan, but he was completely in awe by the civil byplay between them. Even if it was tinged with sarcasm.

He was too choked up to do anything but nod his approval.

It all felt like the opposite scenario to him. That the Sullivans were having dinner and he was the uninvited guest. When he regained his composure, he felt that this was the best acting job ever by two pros who had being doing this sort of thing for a long time. That he was being set up for whatever the reason. Why was the question.

Sargent decided to play along. Just be the dumb flatfoot naive enough to believe they were serious.

"Tully this is all very innocent. Elaine wanted company and talk sports teams in Chicago. That's her passion. I wanted to pick up the tab, but she insisted that she had your permission to use your platinum credit card."

"Perfectly right, Detective. Elaine detests being alone and dining alone, so with my approval she's always inviting a friend to dinner."

"How long will you be spending your vacation in Naples, Detective?"

"Bill, call me Bill, Tully. I'm not on vacation, although with dinners like this it certainly feels like it."

"I'm working. There's some people in Naples, maybe in Pelican Bay, I'm hoping to track down."

"Can we help you with the tracking?"

"I don't think so, because I want to surprise them. It's a Chicago connection. Sort of Chicago business."

"What kind of business is Chicago business, Bill?"

"It won't be a surprise if I tell you, now would it?"

"They don't know I'm visiting, and the people in Chicago that want me to contact them will really make it a wonderful surprise."

"Are they friends or business associates?"

"Sort of business friends that have a great deal in common."

"Well that's great. I hope you find them real quick and have a surprising good time."

"For me anyway, Tully."

"Well Bill, I think I've worn out my surprise, and maybe my welcome, so I'll mosey along and let you two enjoy dinner."

"That's the best news I've heard since you got here, Tully dear. I find it a little awkward trying to seduce the reluctant detective with my husband hanging around."

Sargent gulped hard and virtually spit out the sip of wine he had just taken. He sat up straight and was about to say something when Elaine smiled and said, "jesting Billy Boy. Just jesting. Tully was about to leave. Right Tully?"

"Er...well I...yes, sure my dear. And don't be a bit concerned about my eating. I had a snack before coming here."

"I also know when I'm not wanted."

"So folks enjoy yourselves. Try the Tuscan bean soup, Detective. Deliciozo."

"Hope I see you again. Oh, no, don't get up. By the way, if I can be of help locating your business friends, give me a holler."

While this strange thrust and parry conversation was taking place, Sebastian and Carmen Bach in an adjoining table were all ears. They stared at each other, afraid to breathe, much less speak. "Carmen, Sebastian whispered, don't stare, but that guy in the rumpled dark suit is a Chicago detective. I know him well, because he busted me a few times. I get the drift from their conversation that he's here on police business. If he recognizes me, we're cooked."

"What are you getting at Sebastian?"

"I'm not sure. But whatever, it ain't good."

"I don't understand your drift. What's a Chicago dick doing in Naples on police business?"

"I'll tell you what, he's looking for us. And if he happens to look over here, he'll find what he's looking for."

"Let's not go off half-cocked, Sebastian. There's no way he could recognize the new you unless he knew the old you was now Sebastian Bach. Nobody knows that except the Feds. And they ain't saying a word."

"Sure, and the Feds would never be on Masucci's pad. Eh?"

"And what about the other two, Carm? Have you ever seen them before. At a council meeting or some Masucci July 4th barbecue?"

"Never, nowhere."

"Sullivan? Isn't that an Irish name?"

"How would I know Sebastian, I've lived with guineas my whole life. Names that end in vowels is easy. They're Italian. Anything else is Greek to me."

"Think woman. Didn't Masucci mention that his two best contract hit people were micks. That he trusted them more than those Sicilian morons hanging around?"

"Yeah, I sort of remember that. But those two don't look like hit people. They look respectable. Rich respectable."

"Don't be stupid. That's exactly why they could be hired killers. No one would ever suspect them."

"I'll give you that Sebastian, but it don't make any sense. If they are who you say, what are they doing eating, drinking and socializing with a Chicago detective? Makes absolutely no sense at all unless the cop is on Masucci's pad, too."

"A Chicago cop on the take? My god Carm that would be a first. I would say half the cops in Chicago are on his payroll and new ones added on all the time. That's how the family keeps its operation going."

"I'm sold. So what do you want to do?"

"Get out of here fast, and as quietly as we can. I don't want no Chicago dick getting a good look at this mug, disguise or no disguise. There's too many pictures of me hanging in every precinct out there."

"Oh, that's your guilt speaking, Sebastian. You're not Salvatore Balviano now. I bet your mother wouldn't recognize you. The gray is gone. The mustache hides that scar on your upper lip. Those bottle-shaped glasses hide your black eyes."

"Maybe, but my mother never arrested me. Never grilled me. That dick has, and he's sure to recognize my voice and the one other thing that surely gives me away. I don't even think you know about it."

"No matter, Sebastian. Sit tight. Leaving without finishing dinner would only draw more attention then not. Forget they are there. Capice."

When Tully Sullivan left he walked right by the Bach's table and never looked at either of them. Sebastian with his mouth stuffed with salmon raised a glass of water to his lips, just in case.

The monthly meeting of the MSTBU, the service division of Pelican Bay, drew an inordinate number of people. Over two hundred concerned residents were on hand to hear Sheriff Don Hunter discuss the issue of budget and the handling of security.

Tully sat in the back. He couldn't care less about budget or anyone's personal safety, but would be all ears to what the Sheriff said about how many deputies were deployed 24/7. How many cars? Marked or unmarked? Where? When? What were the vulnerable areas? How security was handled at the Philharmonic?

The questions from the floor were contentious and barely answered to anyones satisfaction. His pat speech and slides glossed over budget and such, but offered high praise for what his department was doing.

People left in droves, Tully as well. He realized he would have to find another source to get his questions answered.

When he returned to his Sanctuary, he placed a call to Chicago for Sergeant Harry Diner at his precinct.

"Sergeant Diner, homicide, can I help you?"

"Yes, Sergeant this is a friend of Mario Masucci. I think you know him, no? He said if I ever needed anything to call you."

"Mario who? No matter, let's not talk on this line. Give me your number and I'll get right back to you."

"Diner?"

"Yeah, now who's this?"

"Not important. Mario said I could get what I need from you."

"Uh, uh, friend. I need some assurance that tells me you're his guy. You could be anyone. IAB or some undercover cop looking to get my badge."

"Need something or this call is ended."

"Well I'm not either. How's this?"

"Me and my partner are the two shooters that your buddy Bill Sargent is running after for those five unsolved hits. The ones on those never closed cold case files. You know Sargent, don't you Sergeant?"

"What do you want?"

"Thank you for your cooperation, Sergeant."

"Don't thank me yet. What do you want is the question? Thank you is not the answer."

"Cleverly put, Sergeant. Cleverly put."

"I want the name of the person on the Witness Protection Program who testified in the first Masucci trial?"

"Salvatore (Shrimpy) Balviano."

"Bravo Sergeant. You've just told me what I already knew. I know all about that grease ball and that he was muscle for the Don. The question that needs an answer is his new name and exactly where he's living in Naples. That ain't too hard to understand, is it Diner?"

"Don't know either."

"Don't know or won't tell? Keep in mind if it's the latter Masucci will be very unhappy with your lack of cooperation."

"I don't know. And that's the honest truth. The Feds are keeping a tight lid on his new identity. I don't think his mother knows his name or where he's living."

"The word is that he's possibly living in a place called Pelican Bay. I'm not even sure that's reliable."

"However, I do have some info about him that might be helpful." "Shrimpy is a big opera lover, If there's opera down your way, chances are he'll go. If you haven't met him, he's a swarthy, muscular guy with gray hair, a scar on his upper lip, deep-set black eyes. His wife is short, with dirty blond hair and big jugs."

"That's beautiful, Diner. You really got it down pat. Did it dawn on you for one minute that the Feds go to all the trouble to give him a new identity and not a new look? You're right about one thing. Even his mother wouldn't recognize him now."

"Dig deeper, Sergeant. I need more info and I need it now. Mario would be most appreciative. Do you get my drift?"

"I'll try, but I can't guarantee anything. Yet there's one other thing about him that might be useful. Balviano used to be a professional boxer. So his brains are a bit scrambled. Look for a guy who walks on his heels and has cauliflower ears."

"I swear if I knew more you'd get more."

"Gotta hang now, too many ears in the area. You'll tell Masucci I cooperated, right?"

Tully hung up.

Bill Sargent was having a crisis of confidence. He wanted retirement in the worst way, but he was still a cop with a job to do. He wanted the two hit people that have kept him in a chase mode all these years. Wanted them real bad. However, all he was doing was treading water. He didn't have a clue what name Balviano was hiding out under. And where. The Sullivans were on his radar as the hit team, but nothing concrete. Only his gold badge instinct told him he was on the right track.

It was a dilemma. They were so ordinary in a right way. They weren't from Chicago. Not a hint of an Irish accent, just Irish names. Hardly conclusive.

So why was his nose twitching every time he thought about it, or came face to face with either of them? This happened in past cases and he was certain it was telling him something this time.

As much as he would like to call it quits and go back to Chicago, he felt it was best to follow his nose and hang around a little longer.

Priorities, he thought. Finding Balviano was his immediate goal. So the first order of business was to check out the opera schedule at the Philharmonic. It's a long shot, he knew, but just might strike gold.

He stopped in the middle of his meandering and screamed to no one in particular. "What the hell am I thinking?"

"Retirement, you idiot. Retirement. That's all I should be thinking. Big deal, finding the hitters and saving Balviano's ass won't change the world one bit. Mob hits would go on, and mob canaries would always be testifying. And the Feds would always be stashing away someone on the Witness Protection Program."

"Screw it all. I'll tell that miserable Captain that I don't have a clue about anything. It's a dead end. And to close the cold case files, or assign nine other detectives if he wants to keep them open."

"Put through my papers, you miserable excuse for a Captain. It's my right. You can't delay it out of spite.

I want to get on with my life of boredom. And with God willing, drink myself to death and join Mary."

A ringing phone jolted him out of his day dreaming. It was Sheriff Hunter with information that two, rather odd Irish characters were registered at the Ritz Carlton. Acting off-the-wall odd. They drank up a lot of Irish whiskey and spoke with heavy Irish brogues.

The bartender got the impression that they were being obviously Irish. Acting kookie just to hide who they really were.

"I know it's not much to go on Detective, but if they are really Irish, maybe it's the two you're looking for."

"Thanks Sheriff. Good job. Hope you're right."

Sargent made a mental note to see the bartender and get some more definitive description of the two oddballs. Maybe, just maybe they were the Sullivans in disguise.

Caught up in the excitement of this tangible piece of information, Sargent forgot calling the Captain, and retirement lost out to being a cop. And since his nose was twitching just thinking of the prospect that the kooks were the Sullivans, gave him renewed hope that he was on the right track. He chuckled to himself that it was so easy to go from the retirement mode, to the very active, investigative cop.

Balviano awoke with a start. Sweat pouring from every pore, soaking his pajamas through and through, creating a pool of water on the sheets.

He looked at the clock and couldn't believe it was only 2 am. It felt like he had been sleeping a week to be so wet. When the fuzziness oozed out of his brain and his eyes were in focus, the events of the dream he was dreaming hit him like a cold, wet towel. This dream was a nightmare that seemed all too real. Maybe too real.

The hit men had broken into the apartment, slashed Carmen's throat and placed the muzzle of a gun in his mouth. He could still taste the metal.

They didn't have masks on, yet he couldn't make out their faces. The tall one with the Irish brogue said if he gave one moments thought to testifying against Masucci it would be his last thought. The quick, painless death of his sleeping wife would be in stark contrast to having his brains splattered all over the bed.

Balviano shuddered with the thought of having his head blown off. "My god it's so real." He tried desperately to see in the dark, to see faces, but only saw shadows and shapes of bodies. Bodies that he saw through.

When his eyes finally became acclimated to the dark the figures were gone. The nightmare remained, indelibly etched in his brain. He reached over to touch Carmen, but she wasn't there. The sheet was soaking wet, even kind of sticky. Panic set in. He screamed out her name.

"Carmen, where are you? Say something. Say something, anything. Jesus, it's true, she's dead. I wasn't dreaming."

In a flash the light went on near her bed. She rushed to his side. "What's the matter, Sebastian? Holy Mother of Mary you're soaking wet."

"Oh, thank god, Carmen, you're alive. Where were you? Why is your sheet soaked with blood?"

"Alive? Blood? Have you been dreaming that dream again? I was in the john. Do I have to announce my coming and going when I'm peeing?"

"See there's no blood. I just wet my pants 'cause I didn't get to the john quick enough. You know my bladder problem. It doesn't always wait for me to make it there."

"Sebastian, stop moaning and look at me. I'm alive. All in one piece. You were only dreaming. Just dreaming."

"Carm, I wasn't just dreaming. It was the most frightening nightmare ever. Real real. They were after me. You were dead, a big smile across your throat, and I had a gun shoved down my throat warning not to testify against Masucci."

"Who was after you? The cops? The Feds? Masucci?"

"No! The two micks. They were right here at the foot of the bed. When I reached over to wake you, there was no you. Just wet, sticky stuff. Blood. It was so very real. And I was next."

"Look around, hon. Nobody is here. The alarm is still set. The doors are locked, The windows closed shut. The drapes still drawn. You were dreaming, Sebastian. Bad dreaming."

"It was real, Carm. I can still sense the danger. They're close by and closing in fast. We're dead ducks."

"Calm down, tough guy. Nobody is close. They don't know who we are or where we are. We still got time to figure things out before you have to testify again. We'll think of something. We gotta."

"Think good thoughts. We've come this far and so far nobody has a clue. Go back to sleep and no more dreaming. We'll talk in the morning."

"No Carm, we talk now. If I go back to sleep the dream, the nightmare will come back. It was telling me something. A warning. My mama, may she rest in peace, use to dream and they always came true."

"What can we do at 2:30 AM, Salvatore?"

"There you made me call you by your right name. I broke the rules doing that. If the Feds knew they would give me five demerits, or take away by beauty parlor privileges."

"It ain't funny, Carm. I'm scared shitless. Me, the guy that broke kneecaps for a living and I'm scared. I can face anything I can touch. I've used muscle my whole life on all kinds of creeps, but it's creepy with ghosts. That's different. I ain't got enough muscle to fight ghosts."

"There's no ghosts, Sebastian. Believe me. Dreams are just that, dreams. Even if they're bad dreams, nightmares, they ain't ever real. Everybody dreams. And lots a times they dream terrible dreams"

"Go change your pajamas, while I change the sheets. Then lights out. I'm still full of sleep."

"What if they come back again, Carm?"

"Break their kneecaps, hon."

"No matter. Think nice thoughts. Sweet dreams."

Sargent sat on a stool at the Ritz Carlton bar, ordered a scotch and soda, then flashed his badge and asked the bartender if they could talk.

"That's what most people do when they sit at my bar," said the bartender.

"Talk. I'm a good listener. Yet why do I think this time things are reversed, you want me to talk and you want to listen. Right?"

"You got it."

"Okay, but first Mr. Detective, there's no smoking in here. Rules you know."

"Oh, it's not lit er..."

"Mike. My name is Mike Halloran."

"Bill Sargent, Mike, and I don't smoke. I just chew on this cheap cigar. There's no law against that, is there?"

"How can I help you detective?"

"The two people you told Sheriff Hunter about. Tell me about them."

"Like what?"

"What did they look like? What did they say? What made you suspicious enough to call the Sheriff?"

"For one they were dressed oddly. To me obviously oddly. The man was a big strapping guy with a weird looking mustache that curled up at both ends. A real wax job. Looked pasted on. Fake. His accent seemed too broad to be anything but phony. I know about accents, as you can tell, since I'm a mick from the old country."

"What did he say, Mike?"

"Nothing about everything. None of which made sense. Without me asking, he said he loved Naples. Thought the weather was perfect compared to where he came from.

Small talk that just seemed like he wanted me to remember seeing and hearing him."

"Drank Irish whiskey like a fish, but never slurred a word. Sat about two hours talking and drinking. Not only to me, but others at the bar. Bought a few rounds for those others. Tipped big, though."

"What about her?"

"Kinda cute, very curvy for an older broad. Lotta hair. Looked like a wig. Wore crazy looking glasses with rhinestones. Made up like circus clown. Flirted a bit with me and other guys at the bar. Spoke loud and fast, with the same phony brogue. Even broader than his. Got the impression she did everything just to be sure she was remembered."

"And made a point to leave before he did."

"They certainly were two doozies. They were really loud and boisterous. Had to ask them to tone it down. I reminded them this was the Ritz Carlton, not some joint."

"Since one of Hunter's deputies told me to be on alert for for any strange people with Irish accents, I felt they fit the bill. Boy they were stranger than strange and so obvious that my bartender's instinct told me they were hiding something or wanted me to think they're not who they seemed to be. I called the Sheriff as soon as he left."

"Did she have a mole on her cheek. Mike?"

"Yeah, now that you mention it, she did. The hair almost hid it, but it was there. Looked like a paste job, too."

"What's with them, detective?"

"Not sure. For the moment it's just a routine inquiry."

"Where are you from, detective?"

"Chicago, why?"

"Well I'm good at accents and felt you must be from the midwest. I came down here ten years ago from Milwaukee. That's not too far from Chicago."

"Good call, Mike. I guess not too many people come from here. Naples seems to be a melting pot. Once here, people stay here."

"I'm curious, sir. What's a Chicago detective doing conducting an inquiry in Naples?"

"Bartenders don't get to ask questions. And if I tell you I might have to arrest you for knowing too much about what I'm investigating."

"Only kidding, Mike. Thanks for your time and the info.

You've been very helpful. Also thanks for the drink."

"Glad to help, but please you don't have to leave a tip."

"One other thing, Mike, if those two show up again call Sheriff Hunter while they're still here. Okay."

"Sure thing, detective."

Sargent stopped off at the Naples Philharmonic box office to check out what operas were scheduled for the immediate future. When he learned that Carmen would be performed for three days the following week, he bought a ticket on a hunch. Hoping that Balviano was thinking along the same lines.

He swallowed hard when the ticket clerk said the cost was $100. Then he smiled to himself. It wasn't his money, but would be charged to the Captain's budget. Opera wasn't his bag, but it would be an enjoyable night out, since it would make the Captain go ballistic when he saw the charge. This would be money well spent.

One week! Ample time to get a haircut, have his suit pressed and shoes shined. The least he could do spending the Captain's money was to look as decent as possible that night, and uphold the reputation that Chicago detectives were one step above plain sloppy.

When he returned to The Inn there was a message from Harry Diner. Urgent. Call ASAP.

"Harry? It's me. What's urgent?"

"Where've you been Bill? Drinking at some bar?"

"How did you know that, Diner?"

"Enough small talk. Give me the urgent stuff."

"The Feds are going to retry Masucci in two months. The word is that Balviano will be brought back to Chicago in six weeks under special guard. Secret, secret."

"What's the hurry? And why so secret?"

"They found out the last jury was bought off, that's why he got off. Now it's doubly critical to have his testimony."

"He will be stashed away until the trial, and the jury panel will be gone over with a fine tooth comb and then sequestered. No names, just numbers. They're going all out to get the verdict this time. They want Masucci bad."

"Yeah, Harry, and Masucci's hit team will know that, too."

"It means they only have a short time to find him and put him in the ground. No Balviano. No damning testimony. No Masucci conviction. So it's crunch time for them."

"Making any progress identifying the hit men?"

"Maybe."

"Any new leads on Balviano's new name or whereabouts?"

"Why?"

"Just curious, buddy. Cop curious."

"Now, now friend. Remember that killed the cat. But no, nothing yet. Not a clue. I do have a sniff of something about the two hired hands."

"Hey, man, that's terrif. The Captain is gonna love that. Can you give me a hint? One cop to another."

"Sorry, but my lips are sealed. No disrespect, my friend, but I ain't giving out nothing to no one. The Captain included."

"It's too sensitive and too important. Getting Masucci is one thing for the Feds to do. Saving Balviano's ass is another thing for them."

"My job is different. Solving the five murders by collaring the two hit men is the only reason I'm in Naples. I want them as badly as the Feds want Masucci."

"That's all I think about. Then retirement is in and my life as a cop is out. And I go out in a blaze of glory."

"The best part, however, is telling our revered Captain to take a long walk off a short pier into Lake Michigan. Boy that would be sweet."

"Gotta go, Harry. Gotta chase those bad guys. Thanks for the heads-up. I owe you again."

"Give my regards to the Captain, just don't mention the long walk. Okay?"

"I hear you, Bill. I'll give him your unconditional love."

"Remember, I'm here if you need help. The hit team or Balviano. Whatever I can do."

"Hi, this is me. I hope that you are you?"

"You got it Diner. Cut out that cute crap. What's up?"

"The Feds are bringing Balviano back to Chitown in six weeks. That's what's up."

"Exact date, Diner. The exact date."

"Don't know. The Feds may not even have set it., No one is talking."

"Masucci says do him now. Don't delay. That's an order from the big man's mouth."

"Get me his name, Diner. Goddamit his name."

"I wish I could help. God knows I've tried, but I've got to be careful. The Feds are very suspicious of anyone nosing around for that info. They're guarding it like Fort Knox."

"I think Sargent knows something or thinks he knows, but he ain't talking. Even to a fellow cop or friend."

"He did mention awhile back something about an opera. Italians love opera. Maybe that helps."

"Forget about music appreciation. Get me that name. Masucci has someone inside the bureau, so work every angle and get me that name. Time is running short."

"Will do everything I can, Tully."

"One more thing, Diner. Get that exact date the Feds will be down here to bring him back. That should be easier push Sargent harder."

"Sounds easy if you say it fast, Tully. The Feds are tough and Sargent is tight as a clam. I'll do the best I can."

"Not good enough. I'm not interested in what you can't do cop.

"You do it or Masucci will find someone else to do his inside work for him. That could affect your bank account, Diner. Or worse case mean a shorter life span."

"Do I make myself clear?"

He slammed the phone down.

The days moved excruciatingly slow. Sargent passed the time watching soap operas, track meets in Australia and reading a mystery novel. He chuckled when he finished the book, simply because the novel was so simplistic, less of a mystery, and more of a joke to a real cop.

The writer made it look so easy. The Inspector character wrapped it up quickly. The clues always fell into his lap. Informants passed on credible tips. Suspects had alibis with holes big enough to allow a truck to get through.

The real killer made obvious mistakes that rarely happen in the real cop world. Exactly 250 pages and he was in custody.

In his world it has taken him five years with not a real, grab-it-with-two-hands clue to get a handle on the hit team. Nobody knows anything. Nobody saw anything. Not a forensic clue anywhere. Fat Shorty's info was vague at best—that Naples was where the action was. The cold case files mentioned that two people with Irish accents were at all the crime scenes. Not a lot to go on. It was better in the book.

He ate a lot of pizza and take out Chinese. Beer bottles were strewn all over. The only other reading he did was the cold case files. He read them over and over. Knew every word by heart, but the only clue (clue?) was the Irish accents.

"The Sullivans," he muttered to himself.

During his sit-in, Elaine Sullivan called five times, but he deliberately didn't return her calls. He had no desire to listen to her mealy-mouthed words of regard for him. Her barely veiled sexual advances. The masquerade was over as far as he was concerned. If they were the hit team, and he was almost convinced they were, the window of opportunity to get them before they got Balviano became narrower.

Diner's latest information made that window narrower than ever. The Sullivans were the end zone, but him finding Balviano before they did was the opening kick-off. He smiled at that one when he realized how often he used football metaphors to make a point. What an influence "da Bears" and Ditka had on him?

The night of the opera, Sargent got to the Philharmonic early and staked out an inconspicuous spot near the main entrance. He had to hope that the Balvianos would enter there, if they came at all. They'll come was all he thought. Instinct. A gut feeling and a little prayer, plus long years on the force made that feeling a slam dunk.

As the hordes of people paraded through the doors, Sargent was overwhelmed by how many were dressed so elegantly, Men in tuxedos and women in long gowns with diamonds dripping from their ears, around their necks and wrists and on more than one finger. He kept rubbing his shoes against his pant leg to get more shine.

When his mind zeroed in on Balviano, he laughed to himself thinking how the Italian muscle man would look wearing a monkey suit. (Like a gorilla with a bow tie.)

The long lines of people presenting tickets made his wait interminable, and he soon realized it would be almost impossible to spot a short, stocky greaseball with cauliflower ears in a monkey suit, escorting a short, round wife with big jugs. Especially with his new face, Balviano would not look like the old Balviano.

For the moment he felt lost, until he suddenly remembered one way he could identify Balviano. One secret locked up in his memory bank, from previous arrests, that could help him pick him out no matter how his face was altered.

The hood had a tic, a jerking of his head from left to right like metronomes, every thirty seconds. There was no way to disguise that. All he had to do was look for a jerk.

Then he laughed out loud at the terrible joke. He was about ready to pat his memory on the back, when he brought himself up short. He hoped no one else had that affliction. It would be embarrassing if he confronted the wrong jerk.

TWO DAYS PRIOR

"Carmen, I know you're gonna think I've lost my mind, but I bought two tickets for the opera Carmen playing at the Phil in two nights. Don't hate me babe. I just couldn't pass up seeing my favorite opera. The Feds putting the pressure on made me throw caution to the wind."

"You know there are two things that make Italians Italian: a good plate of macaroni and the opera."

"Sebastian you've not only lost it, but you are your own worst enemy. How can you forget you're on the Witness Protection Program? That's protection not detection. They can't protect you if you won't protect yourself."

"Aw, come on Carmen, give me a break. Don't be upset."

"Why shouldn't I be upset. You promised. No opera. Nothing Italian. Feds or no Feds. You're not only risking your life, but mine as well."

"Yeah, yeah. I know. I promised that I would never jeopardize your life, much less my own. I figured out how to play it safe."

"We're not gonna sit together. There's gonna be 1500 people there that night. We'll blend in. We can enjoy ourselves this one time."

"That's perfect Sicilian logic, my muscle-bound husband.

We go to the opera together, but don't sit together. I'm one Italian that don't like opera, so I'm just busting out with joy."

"It's selfish, Carm. I apologize. However, I almost don't care if the micks get me, at least I go out with a smile on my face and that great Carmen melody ringing in my ears."

"Wonderful. You go to your maker happy as a lark and I'll be wearing black the rest of my life. If I live that long."

"Salvatore Balviano, I presume? Remember me, Detective Bill Sargent? I had the distinct pleasure of busting you a few times in the past."

"Sorry Detective, I don't think you have the right person. I'm not Salvatore whatever. My name is Sebastian Bach. I've never been to Chicago."

"Who mentioned Chicago?"

Salvatore or Sebastian? Don't matter. I'm not looking to bust you this time for anything, but maybe I can keep you from being whacked."

"Masucci has his two best, high paid killers itching to take you out. And the time is running short."

"Don't turn around. Don't say another word. Make believe we don't even know each other. Read your program. Just listen. I'll do all the talking."

"I think I have a bead on the killers. I know what they look like. They don't know what you look like now. However they're clever. And maybe have some inside info as to your ID. It won't take them long to find out what name you're going by."

"I must admit, that the Feds did a helluva job changing that puss of yours. You almost look like a respectable muscle man. Don't be deluded, paisan. Eventually they'll see right through it. They're very, very good. And very ruthless. They kill for money and that's plain old ruthless."

"Where's your wife, Salvatore? Don't point, just tell me her seat location."

"Does she have a cell phone? When we get out of here, call her and tell her to meet you near the SunTrust Bank right after the second act starts. Don't tell her about me. Capice?"

"Now start walking out. Slowly. Go straight to the bank area. I'm driving a red Buick Riviera."

"And please don't do anything stupid like running away.

"If you want to stay alive, do as I say."

"Just nod."

"Slow Salvatore. Walk do not run out that side exit. Don't look back whatever you do. And try not to look like a hunted animal. Remember this is your life, goombah."

Outside, Balviano called his wife and told her to meet at the bank and not ask any questions.

"How did you find me cop?"

"Opera, Sal old boy. Italians like opera."

"Yeah you got me there, but how the hell did you recognize me? I don't look nothing like the person you collared before."

"Tic tock, Salvatore. Tic tock."

"What the bejesus does that mean?"

"Not many people know you have a tic, an affliction you can't control. It's not on your arrest record, but I noticed it the first time I busted you. I never forgot that tic. I was just looking around for a guy with a jerky head movement."

"You got me there cop. I've had that so long, I forget it's even there."

"Here comes your wife. Just sit, I'll get her."

"Don't frighten her."

"Frighten her? You gotta be kidding. Living with you all these years, living on the edge of the mob world, I don't reckon she frightens too easily."

"Mrs. Bach? Don't be alarmed. I'm a Chicago detective and have your husband in the car behind me."

"What did he do?"

"Nothing. He's not under arrest. Just get in next to him and I'll explain."

"Carm, get in," said Balviano. Don't worry he's not one of the micks. He's a Chicago dick. The one I thought I recognized in Pazzos. You won't believe how he picked me out in a crowd."

"Unimportant, though. He says he's gonna protect us."

"Protect us from who, Sebastian? Masucci? The micks? The Feds?"

"Masucci and the micks are one and the same Mrs. Bach. The Feds only care about his testimony. Masucci and his paid hit men want him dead."

"I want to keep your husband alive, simply because the Feds want Masucci and your husband's testimony will make that happen. My concern is different. I want him alive so I can reel in the two micks. They killed five people in Chicago and I'm here to hunt them down. Your husband is the bait."

"Well that's just ducky detective. You dangle my husband out there and hope they don't kill him before you get them. That's a good plan for you, but really bad for him."

"It's not as bad as you make it sound, Mrs. Bach. I'm not dangling Salvatore any place. Certainly won't jeopardize his life. I just need to use his being here to get the two who I think are the killers to reveal themselves."

"Think? You think? Suppose your thinking is wrong?"

"Then he's out there naked and the real killers get a clear shot at him."

"Maybe you're right, Mrs. Bach, but I don't think I'm wrong about their identity. I just want to be absolutely certain that they're who they are. Then I can go about protecting Salvatore."

"Don't make me laugh, cop. Salvatore means nothing to you. it's those two killers you want for the jobs they pulled off in Chicago. Masucci means nothing to you. And if means sacrificing one of his, a mob guy that is considered dirt to you, you won't give it a second thought. A cop is a cop, and you would give up my Salvatore in a second as long as you nail your killers."

"Ain't that the truth, Detective?"

"I admit, Mrs. Bach, that it may look like that. However, if I didn't care about his living, I could let those killers take him out and then take them in. I don't work that way."

"I want to clear my plate so I can retire in peace, But I won't, repeat won't, put your husband in harms way. In a real sense I can protect him better than the Feds. They won't know who's after him. I will."

"So if you work with me, we can pull it off. I got the two killers in my sights and with the help of the Sheriff's department I can guarantee you 24/7 protection until I slap the cuffs on them."

"Brilliant plan detective. Why don't you put a sign in front of our building that says "Don't Enter", there are people in the Witness Protection Program living in 310."

"Wait a minute Carm, maybe he has a point. Those micks are real good at getting it done, They know about the Feds, but ain't sure they know about Sargent. That could be our ace in the hole to testify quickly in Chicago and get to a place where Masucci can't get us. In and out before the micks can figure it all out."

"Okay cop. Do what you have to do. Just do it right."

"Mrs. Sullivan? Elaine? Hi, this..."

"Bill Sargent, the detective who fell off my radar screen" I'd know that voice anywhere. You've been a bad boy, you never returned my calls. That's no way to treat an admirer."

"Sorry about that nice lady. Didn't mean to be rude, but I have been busy tracking down those two people I mentioned."

"Have you found them?"

"Yes maam. It wasn't easy, but that's why I'm a gold shield detective. Boy were they surprised. I also got a bead on a mob guy we've been looking for since last year. An informant said he was hiding out in the Everglades. Maybe I can make a collar before I go back to Chicago."

"I don't exactly follow, Bill. You were looking for two friends and you located a public enemy?"

"How about that, lady?"

"My, my you are a good detective. But what's this about going back to Chicago?"

"And when?"

"That's why I'm calling. How's your social calendar? And where's Tully these days?"

"What do you have in mind, Mr. Gold Shield?"

"A drink. Dinner. Maybe a walk on your lovely beach?"

"Am I hearing correctly? If I didn't know better, I might think you have romance on your mind?"

"Partly right. A drink or dinner is in order for me not returning your calls. And for all the times you treated me." "The walk on the beach is pure fantasy."

"Yours or mine?"

"Sorry about that. It was a low blow. Thoughtless of me."

"What I really had in mind was dinner with you and Tully. My treat. Want to talk."

"Is he around?"

"Well it was interesting for a moment, Sargent. He's around someplace, probably on the tennis courts."

"I can speak for him, she said rather frostily, where do you have in mind?"

"Our favorite place, Pazzos. Say about 7:00 PM."

"Oh, I almost forgot, may I bring my friend?"

"Male or female?"

"The female variety. Just my old friend that I knew way back when."

One of the two you were looking for?"

"You got it."

"Where's the male of the species?"

"In bed with a cold."

"Well, if you must, Mr. Sargent," in an even icier tone.

"Mr. Sargent? I detect a little coolness there Elaine."

"Just a little. What happened to a romantic walk on the beach?"

"Jealousy doesn't become you dear lady. But just for the record there's nothing going on with me and this lady. I'm merely being an arm for her husband who's under the weather."

"Are we on?"

"Make the reservation."

Pazzos was very crowded, with most of the tables occupied. The Captain said the Sullivans were at the bar and he was holding their table.

Carmen Bach was reluctant to move and Sargent literally nudged her towards the bar. If these were the killers she wasn't sure she could face them. Sargent's broad smile assured her. She felt he read her mind. And then remembered him telling her in the car that they wouldn't have a clue to her real identity.

As they approached the bar, the Sullivans were in an animated conversation. And speaking a little louder than usual to hear each over the noise.

"Elaine, that cop knows something. Why the dinner? And who's this broad?"

"He knows nothing, Tully. Nothing. Just a dumb dick from Chicago. That broad is a friend."

"Sure. And I just picked you up at the bar."

"Tully! Elaine! I hope we're not late. Traffic on 41 was horrendous."

"No, no, Bill. We just got here ourselves. Good to see you again."

"Please meet my old friend, Carmen Bach. Carmen this is Tully and Elaine Sullivan."

"Hi, Carmen," said Elaine. "Have you had a chance to see the opera Carmen at the Philharmonic?"

"I don't like opera."

"I thought all Italians like opera? Although Bach is not an Italian name, you certainly look Italian."

"Half Italian, Mrs. Sullivan. My mother was from Sicily and my father from Lebanon. I guess that's where I got that swarthy look."

"Well in any case welcome to the best Italian restaurant in Naples. U.S.A., I mean."

"And please call me Elaine."

"I'm sorry your husband couldn't join us."

"He's just as sorry. His back acted up on him, so he's resting. Gave me permission to dine out with my friend Bill."

"What'll you have to drink, Mrs. Bach?" asked Tully.

"Carmen, please."

"Sure thing, Carmen. A glass of Chianti? The Reserva is superb."

"Oh, no, I don't like wine, it's too bitter. In New Hampshire we're big on Manhattans straight up with a cherry. Make sure they use sweet vermouth, thank you."

"Chianti, Bill?"

"You know me from the first picture, Tully. That's my favorite dinner drink."

"How long have you known Bill?"

"Long enough. It seems forever."

"What did you say your husband did for a living, Carmen?" "I didn't, but since you asked, he was in charge of accounts receivable, essentially collecting bad debts, for a family owned business in the midwest."

"What exactly does a bad debt collector do?"

"Sebastian was responsible for seeing that people who were late in making payments became current."

"How late?"

"I'm not too sure, but I believe it all depended on the clients relationship with the company. He always told me if someone fell behind more than ninety days, they usually fell further behind or didn't pay at all."

"That's when Sebastian earned his keep. Along with paying up there was interest due on the unpaid balance."

"That sounds like a dangerous job? When one of my customers owed me money, he didn't like being pushed for it. Even threatened to stop doing business with me."

"Your husband must have been a tough guy to deal with those kind of people."

"Sebastian tough? Oh, no, Tully. He was a pussycat. Doing that kind of work for such a long time enabled him to learn the art of gentle persuasion. They actually loved working with him."

"However, he's retired now. It wasn't the bad debt customers that caused retirement, it was the head of the family business. They got into a war of words as to how to do the job best, and Sebastian didn't like doing it his way or else."

"He quit."

"We live a quiet life now in two paradises. Here and in rural New Hampshire. The only thing my husband collects these days are cents-off coupons at Publix Supermarkets"

"Hey while all this talk about bad debt collection is stimulating to my brain, my stomach says it's eating time."

"I'm starved," said Sargent. "Haven't had a bite to eat since breakfast. Busy, busy on the phone with the Captain. He's ordered me back to Chicago pronto."

"Why the rush, what's so important," asked Tully?

"Things are popping all over. All at the same time. There's a new trial coming up soon for a Chicago mob boss where the key witness will have to testify again. He's on the Fed Witness Protection Program somewhere in the South. Everyone in my precinct will be on alert. I probably will be needed there to baby sit the witness until trial."

Also a case I've been working on for five years has gotten some legs. An informant provided some info that the killers of five people are holed up someplace in Chicago. Since I'm the lead detective, it's back to the grind."

"I thought you were on a mini vacation trying to locate your old friends, the Bachs," asked a somewhat unsettled Elaine?

"Partly true. It was a working vacation. What I didn't tell you was that an informant told us that killer or killers I had been chasing for years might be in Naples."

"Proved to be a false lead. But it did pay off in finding my friends."

"So now paradise will be lost for the immediate future. Sunning and funning is out and I have to adjust my mind to the fast pace of the big city. Back to the grind of looking for the bad guys where I always thought they were. And hoping against hope that my retirement comes through before too long."

"I think I talked too much, because I'm more hungry then before. Let's get the chef cooking before they run out of the good stuff."

"Mr. Waiter I think everyone is ready to order. Me first since starving is an understatement."

"Mussels for an appetizer. The house salad, then that great veal chop, medium rare. Oh, yeah, another bottle of Chianti."

"Carmen, have you ever eaten real Tuscan bean soup with clams" asked Elaine?

"Tuscan? Is that Italian? Then the answer is no. I'm a Yankee and that means New England clam chowder. That's how I like my clams floating around."

"Sorry ma'am, that's not on the menu," said the waiter.

"I'm sorry about that, too. So I'll settle for a shrimp cocktail, filet mignon medium well, no potatoes and broccoli. And another Manhattan with two cherries. Thank you."

"Good choices," said Tully.

"My wife and I will have the Tuscan bean soup, the house salad and the veal chop. Mine medium and hers medium rare."

"Now, my here-today, gone-tomorrow detective, what do you want to talk about" piped up a chagrined Elaine?

"Gosh, with all that bad debt stuff and my stomach growling, I've seemed to have lost my train of thought. Probably unimportant.

"In any case it's just nice to spend my last few days in Naples with an old friend and my new ones. Also thought it was a good idea to give Carmen a taste of how the rich and sophisticated live it up in Naples."

"She and Sebastian will be returning to New Hampshire shortly to a somewhat quiet life in a small town."

"Do you have children, Carmen" asked Elaine?

"No unfortunately, but Sebastian is about all I can handle. Since retiring he's like a big kid, always underfoot. He doesn't play golf or have any hobbies, so I'm trying to get him interested in things"

"Like what things?"

"Talking to our local business men about how to run their collection departments, without having to hire lawyers or use the courts. He has a real knack for knowing the ropes and getting the job done. He could help, I'm sure."

"What's his secret," asked an incredulous Tully?

"No secret, Tully. He's just perfected his approach over twenty five years. A direct approach. A convincing one based on fairness. If nothing else, Sebastian was a bulldog who never gave up until they gave in. The check usually was in the mail soon after."

"Very interesting, Carmen. I could have used him when I was in business. Not all my bad debt clients were willing to anything up until I literally had to strongarm them."

"Strong arm them? Physically?"

"No. What I mean is threaten to take them to court. Costly to say the least. I like his method better."

"Does he like anything, asked Elaine? "Baseball, sports or opera?"

"Opera? Not in a million years. Lawrence Welk is his favorite kind of music. Now it's all noise."

"When do you leave Bill," asked Elaine?

"In a few days I think. Just as soon as I get word that the witness is on his way back to Chicago."

"Does that mean, we'll, I will never see you again?"

"I'm sure we'll meet again. Don't know where or when, but it might be sooner than later."

"When my papers come through I'll be on a permanent vacation, my backside on a stool in my favorite watering hole, fishing rod at my side, waiting for the fish to be running in the lake and probably doing a little traveling."

"Naples is a great place to do all three. Might surprise old new friends and drop in on you and Tully."

"We'll be here detective. Just call."

At 7AM there was loud knock on Sargent's door at the inn. Waking from a sound sleep, his first instinct was to reach for his gun. When the knocking got louder, he rubbed the cobwebs from his eyes, and still carrying the gun, stumbled to the door. He looked through the peephole and saw two men in dark gray suits, wearing fedoras and dark glasses.

Even before they flashed their badges he knew they were FBI. He opened the door and when they flashed their badges, he showed them his detective's gold shield.

The stocky one growled, "we know who you are Sargent."

"We have to talk"

"At 7AM? How about later in the day? I'm still not awake or dressed properly for an interview," he said with sarcasm dripping from every word."

"I don't like to talk to the Feds before brushing my teeth and combing my hair."

"Cut the crap, Sargent, we're not here for small talk or that cop sarcasm," said the tall, well-built agent.

"We're to advise you that you're interfering with a Federal investigation."

"Of what?"

"You know exactly of what. It's a crime to out a person on the Witness Protection Program that jeopardizes the trial of a major crime figure."

"I haven't broken any laws that I know of lately. In fact, I haven't told a soul that I've talked to Balviano/Bach. He decided on his own to talk with me."

My job is to get the two hitman that want to get him before testifying against Masucci. For your information they are the same duo that are wanted for five other hits.'

"My job is to keep the killers from making swiss cheese out of the Balvianos."

"First of all, Sargent, we don't care a rats ass about any local Chicago P.D. cases. Our job is to make sure our witness gets to Chicago in one piece to testify. We don't need any help to do that, least of all from you."

"I beg to differ with you my friends. The government lost the first case because the jury was fixed. That won't be necessary this time around when the Masucci hit men kill him. No Balviano testimony. No Masucci."

"What's more you don't have a clue who will execute the execution, so how can you protect him?"

"And you do, Sargent?"

"If that's the case, we have orders from your top brass to pass on that information to us. Immediately."

"No can do, gentlemen. This is my case and the Captain never gave any orders to you. In fact he doesn't give a rats ass about cooperating with the Feds. So you can take your threats and take a hike. I'm going to take a shower."

"Please see yourselves out."

"This is not the end, Sargent. You can't play free lance with the Bureau. We'll have an agent up your rear end every minute of every day until our witness is safely testifying in court. Any further interference from you and we'll arrest you for tampering with a government witness and obstructing justice."

"Is that clear?"

"Perfectly clear. Although your logic escapes me. While you're watching me 24/7, our hit men will be taking out your witness."

"I suggest you leave now or I'll be obliged to call the Sheriff and have you arrested for breaking and entering at this ungodly hour without a warrant, and threatening a law enforcement officer."

"Is that clear?"

"Elaine, he's nailed us cold."

"Who nailed what?"

"Are you deaf and blind? Sargent has figured out who we are. He played us a yo-yo at dinner. Carmen Bach! Would you believe that guinea broad posing as a Yankee.? And her husband a bad debt collector? He was laughing in our face. He took us for the two hicks."

"And did you pick up on Sargent saying the husband had a cold and the broad saying he had a bad back. That cinched it for me."

"I'm not too sure I agree, Tully. She seemed like a nice New England lady. Her food and drink choices were like one."

"New England my ass. She's Italian through and through from the South side of Chicago married to our pigeon, Balviano."

"Sargent got to them first and flaunted them right in our face. That smart-ass bastard."

"Maybe, but I still thinking you're reaching a bit."

"Reaching hell. She practically told us her husband was muscle for Masucci. He was in a family business. Damn right, Masucci's family."

"No maybes, Elaine. Sargent knows who we are and is baiting us with Balviano's wife. He wants us out in the open making a move on that guinea stoolie, then he can move on us."

"That's a little tortured logic, Tully. You're giving a not too bright dick more credit then he deserves. If he's so smart why doesn't he move on us now? Why wait?"

"I'll tell you why. Because he ain't sure. That's why."

"Well maybe not I.Q. smart, but cop smart. He's been a homicide detective a long time and his kind develop street instincts. He smells his prey. And I smell he's ready to pounce."

"Trust me Elaine, I've got street instincts too. Masucci made us rich because I have that instinct for asking big money for our hits."

"And you my dear wife have that natural killer instinct to execute the hits. But sometimes your liking a guy physically let's your women glands get in the way of your brain cells. Sort of clouds your perspective."

"Let me get this straight, Tully. You're the brains and I'm the brawn? That kind of thinking is getting on my nerves. And for a long time now. Masucci believes that you're the "man"...the guy with steel nerves who pressed the trigger on all those hits. Me? I'm just the broad who hangs around for window dressing."

"I'm sick of it, Tully. Not to mention mad as all hell."

"Now hon, you know how the mob thinks: honor, family, loyalty and machismo. The man is the man."

"And you do nothing to set the record straight. Well I want those mobsters to know who is the real man of this team. I want more credit, Tully."

"You get it from me, Elaine. In spades, too. You know my problem. I can't stand the sight of red blood. The color green, as in money, is more to my liking."

"That's gonna change before we finish this job. You're gonna tell Don Mario that my finger has been on the trigger for every hit. I'm the cold-blooded hit man. You're the coward that uses that blood problem as an excuse not to use a gun."

"You tell him Tully, because rest assured I will."

"Look Elaine that's not a good idea. We can't run the risk of blowing a million dollars because your ego is bruised. The Don might take it the wrong way. This is our last hit. Then we can go anyplace, do anything and leave the world of killing, and the mob behind us."

"You want credit. You got it. I'll tell you every day for the rest of our lives how great you were. Are. Promise."

"Don't patronize me, Tully Sullivan. Your Irish charm and Irish bullshit won't work. Not this time. I'm not any sweet, loving, homebody wife, I'm the shooter. The best. We get paid the big bucks because of me. Not because you can negotiate the money deals."

"So as of today, the ground rules will change. You tell Masucci I'm the one that whacks who he wants whacked. And if not, you hit Balviano and I'll collect the money."

"Enough Elaine, get off it. I get your drift. Let's not quibble. You're the best hit man ever. I'm a coward. Only you can put Balviano in the ground, and if it's that important I'll call Masucci today."

"Agreed?"

"So now let's get down to the job at hand. Let's discuss Balviano. What do we know? What name is he using. Where do the Feds have him hiding out?"

"Here's my take. The broad Sargent brought to dinner says her name is Carmen Bach. Interesting name."

"What do you mean?"

"Think about it. Balviano is an opera buff, so maybe they used a classical name like Bach on a whim. Get the phone book and we'll see if Sebastian and Carmen Bach are listed. If so it'll give us their address. We can hit them before they know what hits them and before Sargent has a chance to plan his next move."

"That's thinking like a thick-headed, dumb mick, Tully. If the Bachs are really the Balvianos, that's walking straight into the trap Sargent has set. He wanted that dinner with Carmen Bach and us. As you said, they dropped all kinds of hints that they were the Balvianos. I'm sure he wants us to get their address and go after them immediately. You said Sargent was cop smart. Thinking about it, you were right. He's banking on my making a play for him, our arrogance in thinking we're the best, and years of avoiding arrest when taking out those others, without ever leaving a clue. Somehow, some way Sargent figured it all out and now is casting out his net to reel us in. I guess I really misjudged him."

"If the Bachs are the Balvianos you can be sure he's got them covered every minute of the day. And let's not forget the Feds. We'd be running into a steel trap."

"So my brainy husband, now that we're on the same page, we've got to be smarter and devise a plan to get him outside his fortress, away from his guards, to a place where he's vulnerable."

"Are you talking just to hear yourself talk, Elaine, or do you have a plan rolling around in that pretty little head?"

"Yeah, a plan. Bear with me"

"We invite Sargent and the Balvianos to dinner at our place. Sort of a farewell dinner for our good friend Bill Sargent. He can't refuse that nice offer."

"I can't believe what you're saying, Elaine. We can't hit them at the dinner, without taking out Sargent, too. Kinda risky, don't you think? Might end up with him taking us out."

"I'm not that stupid. Get in touch with your friend Willie the Torch and hire him to torch up the Balviano apartment while they're with us. Then tell him to call 911 and report the fire."

"What about the Feds and locals? How does he get into their apartment?"

"That's why Willie gets the big bucks. He's the best at what he does. He'll find a way."

"What does that do?"

"The Fire Department will contact the Balvianos at our place with the bad news."

"How can you be so sure they'll contact them here."

"I think we know how Sargent thinks by now. He'll be sure to have any emergency call directed to us. Remember, he can't take them too far from the Feds without leaving a number where anyone can reach them."

"The Feds don't have a clue that anyone knows their identity, so Sargent has license to move them around with impunity."

"There's a lot of ifs there, hon. What if Sargent can't convince them to come? What if the Feds won't let him out on the town? What if Sargent has led the

Feds to believe that we're the ones out to take him out?"

"And let's not forget the biggest if. What do we do when we have them here? Fire or no fire. If we don't kill them what the hell do we achieve?"

"Confusion, chaos and displacement. They'll have to find another place to live, and Sargent and the Feds will have to scramble to do it quickly."

"They'll be off guard and so caught up finding that new place that keeping an eye on us will not be on their radar. That's when we strike."

"Where? When?"

"Haven't figured that out yet. But we will know much more then we know now. We'll know for sure that the Bachs are the Balvianos. We'll see what that hood looks like. And we'll find out where the Feds stash them."

"I'm certain that Sargent made up that story about going back to Chicago. He won't make a move while all that chaos is going on. He wants our heads, maybe even my body. This time I'll make it available to him. That'll free you up to take out the Balvianos."

"What? Didn't you hear me admit I'm a coward? I can't do it. It's a psychological blood thing."

"Sorry about that lover. This time you'll have to overcome your cowardice and do the job. Just keep thinking green with the million dead presidents we'll get from Masucci. It will go a long way to help with psychiatric counseling for your problem."

"Jesus, Elaine, I can't do it. So help me I can't do it. Don't make me."

"Yes you can, Tully. You will. If not I'll take care of them myself and make sure there are a few bullets left over for you. This is no idle threat. This is our last job, so it's about time you step up to the plate and swing the bat."

"There's no room for discussion. You do them or I do you."

"Simple."

"Let me sleep on it, Elaine."

"Sleep all you want. Just know when you wake you'll be facing the same dilemma, and maybe a .45 pressed against your handsome face, if you don't have the right answer."

"Tully? Harry Diner."

"Didn't I say never to use my name over the phone you pinhead? What's more never to call me unless it absolutely necessary."

"It's necessary. Absolutely."

"This is direct from the boss man. The Feds are very edgy about what's going on down your way. The word around the water cooler is that the witness has been compromised by our mutual friend, Sargent."

"Compromised? What does that mean? He hasn't made Balviano as far as I know."

"Maybe so and maybe no. They're so paranoid that they have decided to bring him back to Chitown earlier then expected. Secret stuff. No fanfare. No get-out-of-town date."

"Masucci says do him now. And now means yesterday. No more stalling. No more waiting."

"If the Feds are edgy, the Don is jumping out of his skin."

"He says if you can't do it ASAP, then he'll send two of his Sicilian mechanics to take you off the job. And that means goodbye big bucks for you and the little lady. Not to mention putting your own lives at risk for what you know."

"You know the Don. He shows no mercy when somebody doesn't follow orders. Since this directly involves his well being, his lack of mercy knows no bounds."

"Nothing personal, friend. I'm just the messenger."

"Okay, okay, Diner. I get you. But you deliver this message to that greaseball boss of yours: Threats won't get the job done any faster. We have a pretty good idea who he is and real close to where he's holed up. It'll be done in a day or two."

"Also don't call me again, hear? And while you're at it tell Masucci that we don't need any of his muscle to screw up the works. Me and the wife have it under control. Just get the money ready to wire to the Caymans. He won't testify."

"Hello Bill, Diner here."

"Hey Sarge, what do I owe the honor of your call. Let me take a wild guess. Our beloved Captain is going ape over my unlimited expense account?"

"I hope so. Which by the way I've exceeded already."

"He doesn't confide in me Bill, especially about you. However the Feds are going ape over your meddling with someone on their Witness Protection Program. The phone's been ringing off the hook around here. They're furious. And giving the Captain hell."

"Do tell?"

"Yeah, they've complained bitterly to the brass and asked for your head. They're pushing the Captain to get you back here immediately or risk your being arrested. What the hell have you been doing to cause such an uproar?"

"Arrest me? They must be kidding. How can they arrest a cop just for doing his job? I'm tracking down the killers of those five D.O.A's from the past. It so happens they might be one and same that want to take Balviano down."

"That's what I hear the Captain's been telling the brass, but the U.S. Attorney said he'd arrest his mother if she meddled with a Federal witness. Especially a witness testifying against a major crime boss. They want to put Masucci away badly. They can't risk screwing up again, so it's your head on the block, my friend."

"Harry, tell the Captain I'd gladly exchange my head for my retirement going through."

"Not me. You tell him. If I did, he would take my head off."

"Seriously, Bill, the word is out that the Feds want to guard against the unexpected happening and bring back Balviano earlier than planned. They'll stash him at a safe house til the trial."

"How do you know all this, Harry?"

"Mostly grapevine stuff. Some inside info from the Bureau, some CI's on the street and a friend of mine in the mob."

"You're my guy, Bill, so anything that impacts you or your case I make priority number one."

"I thought you told me that the grapevine didn't produce any grapes? You must have had a good growing season."

"I do the best I can, especially for my good buddy."

"What's your mole in the hole in Masucci's headquarters saying about the hit teams moves?"

"They...er...nothing, Bill. Either he doesn't know or ain't talking. Everyone is scared to even mention anything."

"Keep at it Harry. If the Feds are bringing back Balviano sooner than later, maybe he can get a handle on when the hit team is gonna strike."

"Masucci must be telling somebody. I know when he gets desperate he'll yell at all his goons to make sure it happens. He won't care who's listening."

"Will do, Bill, but I can't guarantee anything. As I said, everyone is scared and the word is that nobody is to say nothing about anything. Meeting one's maker is the alternative."

"The Feds have all of Masucci's hangouts wired, but the chatter is only about the next dinner at Ristorante Alfredo. Lasagna and guinea red. That's about it."

"Might be a code for when and where they'll hit Balviano."

"Keep after the mole, Harry. We're close to crunch time."

"Will do, Bill. Gotta go now, I've been on this line too long and the eyes and ears are all around."

"Thanks for the heads-up, Harry.

"I gotta be going too. Meeting with the Balvianos to work out a safety net for them."

"Good idea. By the way, what name are they going under? And where are they living?"

"Oh, Harry, don't ask me anything like that. You know I can't tell you."

"Don't you trust me detective?"

"I don't trust anyone, Sergeant. No offense, but your phone or mine could be tapped and that would be playing god with their lives."

"Bill, this is Elaine. We need to talk right now. Call me when you get back."

"Detective? Sheriff Hunter. Call me when you..."

"I'm here Sheriff. Just screening my calls. What's up?"

"Got some news about..."

"Can it hold Sheriff? I'm on my way to see our favorite Federal witness. Just learned that the Feds will be moving them out earlier then planned. Gotta put my plan in work to trap our two hit men."

"Are your people ready?"

"Ready when you say so."

"However, Mike the bartender at the Ritz Carlton said that the phony Irishman was in drinking most of the afternoon. Said he's had enough of paradise and will be leaving shortly."

"What do you think it means, detective?"

"They're getting ready to blow away our witness before they blow town."

"Was the lady Irish at the bar, too?"

"Never mentioned her, so I guess she didn't show."

"Do you have any idea when they'll make a move? Or where?"

"No, but lady Irish called and wants to talk. I'm sure that's a little smoke screen. Their plan is in motion."

"Let's get ours going, too. Pull out your patrol cars and give them lots of room."

"No surveillance?"

"More than before. Use unmarked cars near them and also close to the Balvianos. Maybe that will fool them into thinking they don't have to worry about us, since we don't know the timetable and they probably do."

"I'll keep in touch, every hour or so. Don't believe anything about anything unless you hear it directly from me."

"Thanks for the Ritz info, and thank the bartender."

"Elaine, this is Detective Sargent."

"My, my Detective, we've gotten so formal."

"You called me, Mrs. Sullivan?"

"Formal and a little frosty too, aren't we Detective?"

"Sorry about that, but I've got a lot to do and little time to do it in. So let's cut the chit chat and talk to me quickly."

"Okay, Sargent, I'll cut right to the chase. I know you'll be leaving for Chicago shortly, so Tully and I want to send you off with a farewell dinner at our place. Bring yYour friends the Bachs if they haven't left already."

"That's a very nice gesture but I haven't..."

"Come on Bill, don't brush me off like that. Do you want me to beg?"

"No. When?"

"Tomorrow at 6:30 PM for cocktails. Dinner promptly at 7:15, in case you have to leave early."

"Tell Mrs. Bach I've ordered in some fabulous New England Clam Chowder from Swans and Tully stirred up a shaker of regular Manhattans. It's on ice as we speak, just waiting for a cherry to be dropped in.

"What does Mr. Bach drink?"

"Milk, one percent fat. He's got a nervous stomach and a weight problem."

"So we can expect you?"

"Thanks for the invite, but let me get back to you in a while. Gotta check with the Bachs. I don't know when they're going back to New Hampshire. Must go."

When Sargent got to the Bach apartment, two FBI agents blocked his way in. Their body language said don't enter. Hands on their weapons spoke volumes: Don't even try.

"Stay where you are, Sargent, said the burly one who questioned him at the Inn. Can't let you in. Orders from the top."

"From the top of what? There are no orders asshole. Get out of my way before I report you to those same people who didn't give you any orders."

"You're on thin ice, Detective. We're here to protect him, and you ain't on any visitors list."

"High-sounding stuff G-Man, but you want him around to testify against the mob. I not only want him to testify, but also to live to testify. There's a huge difference. So get the hell out of my way."

"Hello Carmen. Where's Sebastian?"

"Resting, maybe even sleeping."

"Wake him up and get him in here pronto. We have to talk."

"Let him sleep, Detective, He's having a tough time."

"Sorry about that, but it's important that we talk."

Salvatore Balviano staggered into the living room. A strange look on his face as if he had been wrestling with a bad dream. His ever present tic seemed to be on fast forward.

"Sebastian, sorry to wake you up, But the news I have can't wait. The Feds are moving you back to Chicago shortly. Probably in two weeks."

"Two weeks? What happened to two months?"

"I don't want to alarm you, but they have solid info that the hit team has been ordered to take you out immediately, if not sooner. Masucci is very, very edgy. Doesn't want to take any chance that you get to Chicago and he can't get to you."

"That bastard. I'm gonna fry his ass when I get on the stand."

"That's why the Feds are changing plans. They want you out of here and in a safe place before anyone knows you're not here."

"What'll we do cop?"

"We're going to dinner."

"Are you off your rocker? Eating at a time like this?

"Crazy as a fox, Mr. Bach. In fact we're going into the fox's den."

"I don't follow you."

"The Sullivans have invited us all to a farewell dinner. Not the kind that wishes us bon voyage. They have something else in mind, I'm sure."

"They're going all out in the dinner department. New England clam chowder and cold Manhattans for Carmen. Milk for you paisan."

"Detective is this some kind of sick joke on your part? If so, I'm not laughing. Are you really trying to protect us or get us killed, "asked Carmen?

"To the contrary, dear lady. We'll be setting our own trap by keeping them right in our sights. They won't dare kill anyone at dinner, but we'll find out what's on their mind."

"For starters they want a good look at the new Salvatore Balviano. The rest will surface when they ask questions."

"It's better that we go to their place and know what to expect, rather then them coming to your place when you least expect it."

"Now, am I making any sense?"

"Besides I'll taste everything first to be sure that poison is not their weapon of choice."

"Still not laughing, cop. Sebastian and me ain't going anyplace without an army of cops. Those two are loose cannons and I ain't giving them an easy shot at us."

"Carmen, trust me. Nothing will happen at dinner. You'll have an army of cops right with you. The Feds will wiretap the place and hear every word. At the first sign of trouble they'll be in the place. The Sheriff's deputies will be covering the roof and every entrance and exit."

"I still don't like the smell of the whole thing" said Carmen.

"The cop is right, Carm. I like what he's saying. I like someone who wants my bones standing right in front of me. They may be the best Masucci has, but I was pretty good in my day. They don't scare me one bit."

"Besides, I'll be packing heat myself."

"Cool it, Sebastian. You won't be packing anything. The only one with a license to carry and kill is me."

"We'll eat and enjoy and make believe we don't know a thing."

"I know you're tough Sebastian, but this time I want you to play dumb, be meek as a lamb. Forget you were a hood, and play the retired New Englander for all it's worth. Capice."

"My guess is they'll reveal their hand during dinner. It may be subtle, but I'll catch its drift. Just believe in the end we'll get them before they get you."

"Yeah cop, that sounds good if you say it fast, but it's my ass on the line. And even if we get them out of the way, what makes you think Masucci is not gonna whack me in Chicago? Eh! He don't want to go to the joint. No way."

"Only the Feds know the time table, Sebastian. They ain't telling anyone. And when you get there you'll have cops virtually sleeping in bed with you."

"Don't blow smoke at me, Sargent. Don't think for a second that Masucci doesn't have a cop, with my name on a bullet, who'll be sleeping in that same bed."

"He's the Don, remember? He owns the town. Everyone, and I mean everyone, is on his pad. Top brass in every precinct. Detectives. Beat cops in neighborhoods where he does most of his "business". Assistant DA's. Judges. Yeah Judges. And even Feds."

"He doesn't head the most ruthless and profitable family in town by leaving any stone unturned."

"My life will still be up for grabs no matter how many G-men and cops are all around me."

"You're probably right, paisan, but you decided to sing to get immunity. So you have to be ready to take the risk."

"When it's all over, and Masucci and others in the family go to the joint, you'll have the rest of your life to live without fear. With money, a new name, a new address where no one will ever find you."

"That's the only way to look at it."

"For now, however, we go to dinner tomorrow. This cop is taking every precaution to keep you alive in Naples, as well as back in Chicago. And making sure the Sullivans go back in cuffs."

"Not thrilled, Detective, but I don't have a choice. Do I?"

"When is this god-forsaken dinner?"

"Tomorrow, 6:30PM for cocktails. Pick you both up at 6:20. Wear nice clothes. Whatever you do don't mention anything about opera."

"Detective Sargent? This is your Captain. How many times do I have to call you before you return one of them?"

"I've been very busy chasing down the bad guys, Cap. What's up?"

"That's my question, you broken down lush and excuse for a detective."

"Not much. Just chasing."

"Are you playing games with me, Sarge. Sgt. Diner tells me you found the two killers. Why aren't they in cuffs on the way back here?"

"Diner told you what? How does he know? I never told him a thing."

"Don't lie to me. Bring them in Detective. Now. Or else I'll have your badge and you can kiss your pension goodbye for dereliction of duty. Do you hear me?"

"Hear you? I'd hear you without a phone. Diner must be on drugs. As of this moment, 8AM today, I don't know if the two people I've zeroed in are the hit men. By tomorrow that might change."

"In any case, if you don't approve the way I'm handling this, take me off the assignment and put my papers in. I sure would appreciate it, Captain sir."

"If not stay off my case and let me do my job. I'll do what I have to do the best way I know. Job one is to get them before they get the Fed witness. Then you'll have them tied up in a nice little ribbon for those five other hits."

"And if my papers are not in when I get back, I will kick your ass up and down State Street."

"Got that, sir? Don't call me again."

"One more thing, tell my "friend" Diner not to call me either. If I were you, I'd look into his comings and goings. Check his phone logs, too. You might find Masucci's private telephone number on his speed dialing."

"Sargent? This your favorite drinking and dining companion."

"What the hell do you want now, Elaine?", somewhat exasperated.

"Now, now Mr. Independent cop, Don't get your dander up. I can't wait 'til tomorrow to see that puss of yours. Tonight seems to sound better."

"With or without Tully?"

"No Tully. He's in Fort Lauderdale. Has an investment fire to put out there. So be a nice boy and say yes. I have a couple of prime steaks raring to be grilled and a very good bottle of Chianti Reserva waiting to be uncorked."

"How's that grab your taste buds?"

"Sounds like you have more than eating in mind?"

"Am I that obvious?"

"Just a little. It's mostly the heavy breathing I hear that makes me get the whole picture."

"Well now that you have the picture framed, what say you? 7PM is good for me. I'll be wearing something very comfortable. No suit and tie, please. Very casual. The less the better."

"I didn't hear me say yes, Mrs. Sullivan."

"I know, but I didn't hear you say no."

"Okay, we're on lady. I guess I'm just putty in your hands. Please keep in mind that the heavy breathing and your sexual inferences are not as half attractive as the steak and Chianti Reserva."

"I read you. Just you keep in mind that's only the appetizer. Dessert might be a little more appetizing."

"Mr. Tully Sullivan, please. Thank you."

"He's not in. Who's calling?"

"Sgt. Harry Diner of the Police Department."

"Sorry we don't pledge anything to the Police Pension Fund or whatever over the phone. Send us the paper work and we'll consider."

"This is THE Tully Sullivan residence, no?"

"We've been through that officer. What do you want?"

"I'm not calling for any contribution. In fact, I'm about to make one to you. It's free lady and might help you execute your job better and sooner."

"I'm Sgt. Harry Diner of the Chicago Police Department."

"That's what you said before. Except now it's Chicago."

"What I didn't say was that we work for the same boss."

"We're retired and don't have any boss, Sergeant."

"I respect keeping your cover Mrs. Sullivan, but let's stop fencing. Time is running out and this is no time for games. I've spoken to Tully before and he knows I'm on Masucci's payroll."

"The Don is getting edgy now that he's found out that the Feds are bringing back Balviano earlier then planned. He doesn't want him back on two feet. That's the message he wants me to convey to you."

"Mrs. Sullivan? Are you still there?"

"Hanging on every word, Diner. I'll tell Tully when he gets back. Meanwhile you convey this to Masucci: not to worry. The job will be done in a few days."

"Also convey to him that we don't need no dirty cop telling us how to do what we do. Crawl back in your hole, Diner, and lose our number. Got it?"

"A warning to the wise-ass, smart lady. Don't underestimate my good friend Bill Sargent. He ain't as dumb as he looks. For my money he's the best homicide cop in our town. And dangerous when he acts his dumbest."

"So I repeat. Just a few days, Mrs. Sullivan. That's all you got. Masucci also wanted me to convey that if not, he'll send two other mechanics to take over and do your job. Maybe have to do a job on both of you. The money ain't in the bank yet, lady."

"Bug off, you excuse for a vermin."

"Come in Bill. The door's open. Pour yourself a drink."

"Tully? What the hell are you doing back so soon?"

"It's my home, too, wife. And what are you doing in that sheer negligee?"

"Don't bother to answer. I guess Bill is our Bill. Is this your time for a romp in the hay with our illustrious detective friend?"

"Get out of here, Tully, and quickly. Sargent could be walking in at any moment. He's not expecting to see you. You knew that we were getting together. Get out before you ruin everything. I told you about tonight, didn't I?"

"Yeah, you told me. Didn't necessarily listen. And I definitely don't have to like it."

"Like it or not Tully. The plan is the plan. The end justifies the means even if it bruises your male inflated ego. We have too much at stake for you to let Mr. and Mrs. get in the way of a million bucks."

"Be a big a boy and scoot out of here or everything we've worked out will be in jeopardy."

"I don't have to like it, Elaine. What husband would?"

"That's enough. Go Tully, don't make me tell you again. I have too many things on my mind to worry about my petulant, jealous husband."

"Especially with the call I just received from Chicago."

"The heat is is on and we have to move on Balviano in a few days."

"What heat? From Masucci?"

"No. A Sgt Diner with a rather threatening message from Masucci."

"I told that low-life cop not to call unless absolutely necessary. What was the threat?"

"The Don wants Balviano dead ASAP or he's had it with us, and will send two of his goons to do the job and probably take us down, too."

"He said that? That's not a pleasant thought."

"Brilliant deduction. Hitting us is not the most unpleasant part of the threat. Losing out on one million dead presidents is an excruciatingly painful thought."

"So go and we'll discuss this later."

"Alright. Everything is a go with Willie the Torch. See you later, wife. Try not to enjoy it too much."

"Come in Bill, the door is open. Pour yourself a drink, while I pour myself into something more comfortable."

"Do you always drink milk, Mr. Bach, asked Tully, even if you're eating lasagna?"

"I don't eat lasagna, Mr. Sullivan. I don't like eyetalian food. Scrod, Maine lobster, fried clams and good old Yankee dishes are my favorites."

"Oh, goody. Then you're going to enjoy my special recipe New England Clam Chowder, said Elaine Sullivan. Got it from an old sea captain when we visited Cape Cod."

"May I call you Sebastian? Hate to be formal when I have guests for dinner."

"Sure Sebastian is okay. And Carmen will be very happy. New England Clam Chowder is her favorite. Lucky guess that you should make that."

"Not really. Carmen told me it was her favorite when we had dinner with her and Bill at Pazzos."

"Just curious, though about your names. Bach and Carmen. You must be opera buffs."

"Opera? Ain't ever seen one. Don't think I'd like all that foreign stuff."

"Well Tully, Elaine, while we're mentioning favorites, this Chianti Reserva is mine. So I'd like to toast you for being such gracious hosts, and also my good friends, The Bachs, who'll be leaving Naples shortly for home."

"It's been a long time between seeing each other and now it seems like it will be a long time before we meet again with me going back to Chicago. Don't forget to write."

"Saluté to all."

"Very nice, Bill. And in the spirit of toasting, I'd like to offer one to our friend Detective Bill Sargent. Both Tully and I have enjoyed your company and wish you well on your forthcoming retirement."

"Now with all the toasting out of the way, let's drink the wine and let's eat. Everyone must be starved."

"Tully answer the phone. It might be the call you expected from Ft. Lauderdale?"

"Hello. This is Tully Sullivan. Who? Oh, yes Detective Sargent is here. What? A fire? Where? Do you want them or the Detective? Hold on, I'll get him."

"Sargent, it's the FBI. There's been a fire at the Bach's apartment. Want to take it or should Sebastian?"

"The FBI? Why me, and why Sebastian?"

"I don't know, but they asked for him?"

"I'll take it Sargent. This is Bach. What the hell are you talking about a fire?"

"What were you guys doing? Who's in charge? Put him on."

"Tell me how this could happen with you guys right there? That's no excuse. No, not later. We'll be right over."

"Uh, we can't get in? You're investigating what? It's been totally burnt out? You think it was deliberately torched? By who?"

"This is some kind of sick joke you're telling, right? It's not? So what the hell were you guys doing protecting me?"

"Sure, sure. You were on the job. Sleeping on the job is more like it. Well if we can't get in, where can we go? Okay, pick us up, we'll be downstairs in the lobby of the Sanctuary."

"Ten minutes? Make it five you knucklehead."

"Hold the phone, Sebastian, said Sargent. Don't say another word. Hang up now."

"What's going on Bill? asked Elaine. Why would the FBI call the Bachs about a fire in their apartment? The FBI, not the Fire Department? I don't understand?"

"That's a good question Elaine, said Tully. I guess the Bachs must be very important people if the FBI is involved. No?"

"The party's over, yelled Sargent. We gotta go. Right now. Nice work Mr. and Mrs. Sullivan."

"Nice what Sargent?" said an almost smiling Tully.

"The dinner. It was a nice gesture. A perfect going away."

After everyone left, Tully and Elaine did a little Irish jig around the apartment. They couldn't conceal their joy over what they accomplished. Out came a bottle of Irish whiskey, and Tully toasted the brilliance of his wife.

"You did it, baby doll. Flushed them out and made our job easy."

"Elaine did you see the face job the Feds did on that hood. He almost looked normal. Must of cost a fortune. I wonder if they had to shoot the plastic surgeon?"

"The dinner was a great idea, Now we know what we're looking at when you blow away that new face."

"First thing tomorrow, my dear wife, I'll speak to my guy inside the Fire Department and find out where the Bachs are being relocated. That fire will be the last big event in their lives before their flame burns out."

"Very poetic, Tully. Very poetic. Didn't know you had it in you."

"Thought you might like it. Every now and then I call on the muse to express my inner thoughts. The truth be known, however, I read that very line in a poem written by an anonymous poet."

"Now throw out that New England Clam Chowder gop and let's get a red-blooded American steak at Andres."

"And a stiff drink, Mr. Muse."

"Good idea, but make it a bottle of champagne."

When the Bachs and Sargent arrived at the apartment, they were met by Sheriff Hunter. Consternation was etched on his face. He took Sargent aside and whispered, "it was an inside job, Detective."

"No kidding," he said. It's an apartment, not a goddam forest where lightning strikes."

"No. Not an accidental inside job. Somebody got past those Feds and torched the place. A professional arsonist."

"I know what you meant. I'm just pissed off enough to be a little sarcastic."

"How could those arrogant Feds let somebody into their apartment? Watch dogs my eye, they were plain dogging it. Probably were having a drink someplace. Or watching the broads at the pool."

"In any case rank incompetence or worse yet the mob got to them."

"Incompetence, Detective. Complacency at best. They might have been lulled into a false sense of security. The Bachs were with you, and the thought that somebody might torch the apartment was never given a thought."

"Either way, Sheriff, they didn't do their job. It's up to us to clean up after them."

"Keep an eye on the Bachs, I'm going in to take a look."

"You're not going anyplace, Detective," said the agent in charge who was standing by the door. It is a crime scene, and under Federal law is under our jurisdiction. Nobody gets in except our forensic investigators."

"Get out of my way, said Balviano, I'm going in. It's my apartment and you or nobody can keep me out. I had some very valuable papers and family things that maybe the fire hasn't destroyed."

"And what's more, if you're so vigilant now, where the hell were all your people when that guy was putting a match to the joint.? Eh!"

"Cat got your tongue, G-man. Get the hell out of my way." Sargent jumped in and grabbed Balviano, stopping him at the doorway.

"Cool it, Salvatore. There's nothing left inside that's more valuable than your life. We're leaving right now. The killers had your apartment torched to get you out in the open, where you'll be fair game. And now that they know what you look like they'll zero in on where you'll be going and that makes their job that much easier."

"Where are you taking us?"

"To my place. Get in the car, both of you. Don't waste a moment, because the micks could be watching our every move."

"Sheriff, be sure no one tails us when we leave. Block off all the streets. We'll be at the Inn. Call you later."

"Hold it right there, Sargent. Where do you think you're taking my witness?" as he pulled out his gun and pointed it at his head.

"Now that's not a smart move Mr. G-Man, 'cause if you're not ready to use that thing on all of us, get out of our way or that gun will be shoved down your throat."

"You're breaking a Federal Law, Sargent."

"Thank your lucky stars I'm not breaking your arm for pulling a piece on a cop."

"Where are you taking the Balvianos?"

"It's on a need to know basis, and I don't see your need to know. Move it."

"He's our witness. We have jurisdiction."

"Jurisdiction, maybe, but possession no. There's a leak in your rowboat, so my possession has jurisdiction over your jurisdiction. Got that? You'll get them back when it's time to go back to Chicago."

"Tell your bosses that I'm joined at the hip with the Balvianos and will protect them until I get the killers."

"I'll keep in touch. Don't try and call me. I'll call you."

Sargent drove north towards Bonita Springs on 41, made a U-turn then west on Wiggins Pass, back to 41, then east to Airport-Pulling, then east on Pine Ridge Road to a motel near I-75.

The Balvianos sat in the back quietly watching Sargent juking and deking to be sure he wasn't tailed.

After checking in, in the privacy of the room he emphatically told them not to open the door for anyone. Not to use the phone. Not to go outside for any reason. "I'll call every hour or so, he said, but don't identify yourself. Wait to hear my voice. Capice, Salvatore?"

"Yeah, clear cop. How long do we stay in this dump?"

"We'll be on the move tomorrow. Keep that door locked."

"What about something to eat? We're hungry. Didn't eat much at the mick's place."

"I'll get food to you shortly. The messenger will give you the password WP to be let in. Under no circumstances allow him in without giving the password."

"Tell me cop, why you're doing all this for us? We're not your problem. Taking on the Feds, too."

"It's not because I like you Balviano. You're still a mobster in my eyes, the kind I've been rousting my entire cop life, but my problem until I know you're safe from the hit duo. It's self-serving for sure, but I've been after them for a long time for five previous hits. And nothing would make my retirement more perfect then to have them on a gurney with a needle in their arms."

"You're driven by this, ain't you?" asked Carmen

"You might say that, Mrs. Balviano. Cops don't like killers getting away with murder. Those two have had me flailing away, chasing ghosts for years. Now they're finally in my sights, and I'm gonna take them down. The only thing I'll be chasing for the rest of my life will be fish in Lake Michigan."

When he got back to the Inn, Sargent stopped at the bar for a nerve-soothing drink and some nothing conversation with the bartender. He felt worn to a frazzle with all that happened that day. He checked his watch and realized that time was flying by. It was almost 8PM. He got the phone from the barman, called the China Pavillion and ordered wonton soup, egg rolls, spare ribs and Chicken Chow Mein for the Balvianos. Gave them his credit card number, said he was a Police officer, and requested the delivery man use the password when making the delivery. He made a mental note to call the motel from his room. After an hour of nothing conversation, Sargent finished his second drink and got in the elevator. A hot shower was his next move, followed by a 30 minute snooze.

Sargent opened the door of his room and immediately sensed something didn't feel or look right. The place was dark and he was certain he left the desk light on. There was music coming from the radio at peak volume. Funny, he thought, it was never turned on. The drapes were drawn even though he always opened them the minute he opened his eyes after waking up. The hair on his neck was tingling. He reached for his gun, as he turned on the desk light, only to be faced with the muzzle of a .38 Smith and Wesson. The face behind the gun was his "friend", Sergeant Harry Diner, with a maniacal look in the form of a smile.

"Drop the gun Bill and sit down. Slowly with that piece. No false moves."

"Masucci, Diner? Kinda felt all along, with all your being curious, that you were on somebody's pad. Masucci makes sense."

"You know how it is? Can't live on a Sergeant's pay, Sarge. Mama needs new shoes. Lots of them. Old Harry likes flashy cars."

"Okay, Harry, now that we've discussed your budgetary needs, what do you want from me?"

"I don't want to have to kill you, so here's what the boss man wants you to do. Catch the first plane back to Chicago and forget the Sullivans ever existed. Once they do the Balvianos, Masucci won't care diddly-squat what happens to them. You can bust them, make cop of the year, and maybe pick up a few sou from the Don as a thank you."

"He'll be happy as a pig in slop, because without Balvianos testimony, he never gets to have a trial again."

"Cop of the year? Sounds enticing."

"Then you'll do, Bill?"

"No can do you rat fink. Whatever you and the Don have worked out, won't work. The Sheriff knows the Sullivans are the hit team and will grab them immediately if I don't speak to him every hour on the hour."

"Make it work, Sarge. Call and tell him that you've been called back to Chicago. They got the real killers and the Sullivans are not hit men."

"No can do either. I had a hunch that someone would do exactly what you want me to do, so the Sheriff and I worked it out that if I told him anything like that, it was because I was under the gun. The Sullivans will be arrested as fast as you can say Harry Diner."

"Then you die, Sarge"

"I don't think so "friend". Don't think so. You or the Sullivans don't have a clue where I've stashed them. No Balviano. No hit. The Sullivans get busted or whacked by Masucci's gorillas. Then he'll be looking for your head. It's a lose lose situation, Harry."

"So go ahead, pull the trigger you snake-in-the-grass or else I'm going to take it from you and beat you to a pulp with your own piece."

"Shoot, Diner. Remember we both know what a sniveling coward you are, and have been your whole life. I don't think you have the balls to take me out. In fact your hand is shaking more each second."

"Shoot, Harry baby or walk out that door. Just don't let it hit you in the ass on the way out. Tell The Don the Sullivans will be back in Chicago in handcuffs before the Feds bring back Balviano to testify."

"The trial will be on. Salvatore Balviano will sing his heart out and your meal ticket will spend the rest of his miserable life in a suit with different stripes. In a room smaller than his clothes closet at home. His only companions will be prison guards who don't speak Italian. And what's more he'll never taste lasagna again."

"Tell him all that with my compliments."

"Goodbye, Harry. I'm going to take a shower. Enjoy your flight back."

When he heard the door slam shut, Sargent heaved a sigh of relief. Composed himself. Realized he was shaking as much as Diner, and called Sheriff Hunter.

"Pick up a cop named Harry Diner at the airport. No special treatment, just throw him in a cell until the Sullivans are busted."

"What did he do, Bill?"

"Tell you later."

Then he took a shower.

"Detective? It's Sheriff Hunter."

"Good news, Sheriff? You got Diner in custody?"

"Not exactly, Detective."

"You saw him at the airport, yes?"

"Yes, my men saw him."

"So what do you mean not exactly?"

"We saw him alright in his car at the back of the terminal. He had eaten his gun."

"God almighty, that's terrible. A good cop gone bad."

"What do you mean?"

"He was on Masucci's payroll and doing everything possible to prevent me from wrapping up the Sullivans."

"I was trying to save him from himself. Didn't work out."

"I guess he felt it was easier to blow himself away rather then have to face a department investigation or end up in Lake Michigan wearing cement shoes."

"Thanks Sheriff for everything. You and your men have been a great help. However, this is not the end of anything, it's only the beginning. We've got lots of work to do in making sure the Balvianos are safe and the Sullivans locked up."

"What's your next move, Detective?"

"For the moment they're safe, but I'll let you know when and where I'm moving them. You keep a close eye on the Sullivans and let me know immediately when they're on the move."

"Lemme speak to Tully Sullivan, lady, the boss is calling."

"What boss? And who is this?"

"Don't waste my time, lady, put him on. And now."

"This is Tully, who's calling?"

"Hold for Don Masucci."

"Sullivan, what's going on down there? Why haven't you taken out that vermin Balviano yet?"

"Er...its...well Don Masucci we just got a look at what he looks like now and where he lives. The Feds fixed his face over and had him pretty well hidden. But we got him in our sights now and you can bet your last dollar he'll be toast in the next day or two."

"I promise."

"Promises don't get it done, Sullivan. And it's not my last dollar you should be concerned or worried about. I'm paying lots of bread to kill that traitor, not promises. And I can promise you that if it ain't done in the next few days, you can kiss that money goodbye. You also might consider moving far away, far away in case some of the council think you both should be taken out instead. I'm not going to prison. Do you read me?"

"Listen here, Masucci, this is Elaine Sullivan", virtually screaming into the phone. "Don't you threaten us. We've done your dirty work for years, and did it well. Nothing was ever traced back to you. We're pros Masucci, the best that money can buy. Don't ever forget that. We'll get that slime bag without your not so subtle reference to hitting us. So lay off."

"Sullivan, listen up. Get that broad off the phone. Tell her to show respect."

"Two days, two days. That's it. Or else."

Steaming mad, Elaine Sullivan slammed down the phone uttering every profanity she could think of. Tully did the same. However, they realized they didn't hang up on the Don, since he had done so moments before.

Without saying a word to each other, Tully phoned his contact in the Sheriff's department to find out where the Balvianos were hiding out. He was told that nobody, including the Sheriff himself, had a clue, but the Chicago cop would be moving them soon and would notify the Sheriff when and where. The Deputy promised to call Tully immediately.

"Elaine, we've got to be ready to move on a moment's notice. Sargent will keep moving them around 'til the Feds move them back to Chicago. You heard the man, time is running out."

"Listen carefully, Tully. That greaseball Masucci doesn't scare me one bit. We'll do the job, collect our money and then tell him to screw. I couldn't care less whether or not he rots in jail. I just want my payoff."

"You may not be scared, but I am. Those mobsters show no mercy. So if I were you, I'd can the tough girl act and think about what we do next."

"You're right. I just don't like being pushed around, much less threatened, by an uneducated Sicilian."

I have a plan that I've been thinking about. Want to sleep on it."

"Can you give me a hint, maybe I can help.?"

"Not yet. Let me work it out in my mind then I can run it by you. Let's hit the sack."

"Bill? Elaine Sullivan. Did I wake you?"

"No. The phone ringing did that. What time is it?"

"Two AM."

"Two AM! Why the hell would you call me at this god- forsaken hour? I just got to sleep two hours ago. Be a nice girl and call me later when I'm awake."

"Gotta talk now Bill."

"Are you home? Where's Tully?"

"Out."

"Out? At two AM? Out where?"

"Don't know and don't care. Probably wandering, looking for a bar. We had an argument about nothing."

"Alright, now that I'm half up, what do you want to talk about?"

"I'm concerned about the Bal...The Bachs. How are they doing? Did they find a place to live?"

"Why the sudden interest in them?"

"I feel badly for them. Being burned out of their home. They're such nice people. Down home people. I was just curious about their predicament."

"I bet you are."

"What did you say? I didn't catch that."

"Nothing important. My tongue isn't fully awake yet, so I probably was slurring my words. I'm sure they'd be grateful for your concern."

"Have you spoken to them? Do you know where they are?"

"No and definitely no. They may have left for New Hampshire."

"What about their personal things?"

"Gone, all gone up in flames. The good news is that they were only renting. I'm sure they feel extremely fortunate they weren't in bed fast asleep when the flames were running all over the place, destroying everything. Lucky that they're alive. Clothes and stuff you can always replace."

"Now, Mrs. Sullivan, that we've covered the saga of Bachs, why did you really call at this ungodly hour? My eyes are still only half open."

"I should have known, Bill, that you can read me like an open book. I was making small talk "til I felt comfortable getting to my real reason."

"I have a proposition for you."

"Mrs. Sullivan. Mrs. Sullivan. This early in the morning? My brain is not fully awake, much less the part of me that gets up much later."

"No matter, please save your propositions for Tully."

"That's what this is all about. I'm leaving Tully and want to be with you, if you'll have me. Not talking marriage yet. Just being together."

"I'm terribly attracted to you and Tully knows it. That's what we've been arguing about for some time. We've been drifting apart because of our different interests."

"He's a weak man all wrapped up in himself. Lots a time for tennis and little time for me. I need a strong, sensitive, caring man who understands my needs."

"That's very flattering, Elaine, but you've got the wrong guy. One, I'm not available."

"You're seeing someone? Is it serious?"

"You might say that."

"And two, I'm a former fall down drunk always thirsting for that next drink. And in weaker moments falling prey to the idea that one drink can't harm me."

"Besides that I'm very cynical about the world. Just too many murders, kidnapping, rapes and other violence. After 25 years of being part of that carnage, I have only one goal the rest of my life, and that's to retire and stop chasing the bad guys."

"Strong I'm not. I try to hide it with a certain kind of bravado, but I'm weaker then your perception of Tully. Sensitive? Hardly. Cops ain't very sensitive. We develop a tough skin seeing so many horrendous things, not to mention the terrible people involved."

"As for caring? Talk about selfish. I care only about my next drink and my trusty fishing pole."

"So Mrs. Sullivan, that's my roundabout way of saying thanks, but no thanks."

"What if the proposition comes with divulging a secret?"

"A secret about what?"

"A secret that you've been trying to get your arms around for years. Can you keep one?"

"If I'm sober maybe. If I'm drunk highly unlikely."

"Well I hope you're sober and even if your eyes are half closed, I hope your ears are wide open."

I know you've been looking for two mob hit men for years. Tully and I are the two."

"I don't think you're surprised, simply because you figured that out awhile back."

"Keep talking, lady."

"That's it. We whacked those five in Chicago and now we're pointing a loaded gun at our next target: The Balvianos. Your so-called Bach "friends" from New Hampshire. That was the thinnest veiled cover I ever heard."

"Tully wasn't convinced that you had us pegged for the hit team. I knew different. I knew that you knew, almost from our chance meeting, and was playing a little game with us 'til you were absolutely sure. All the time probing. Probing. Trying to draw us out to say something that would be proof positive."

"I tried all my tricks to seduce you and distract you, but you wouldn't bite. Sort of deflated my ego. It was very clever of you to say you were looking for two old friends, when you really were searching for the Balvianos. Nearly had me convinced."

"By the way, how did you ever find them?"

"Tic, tock. Tic tock."

"I don't understand?"

"Don't even try. It's an inside joke between me and myself."

"You're good, Bill. For a long while I didn't understand you period. What you were doing, what you were thinking? What you felt about me? But mostly wondering if you made us? I realize now that you didn't move on us because we didn't make the Balvianos. Smart and patient."

"Well the cat and mouse game is over. You found them and made sure we got a good look at them. Our plan was to smoke them out with a fire, but once again you were a step ahead. If there was an emergency the Feds would call our place."

"We got them out of their apartment, but once you made us for sure, you got them away from us. Now we're scrambling to find them again."

"What is Tully really doing?"

"He's on the prowl. Checking his informants in the FBI, the fire department and the local Sheriff's department. The man spreads the wealth around."

"He's got an itchy trigger finger. Always did. For the record, he was the shooter in all five hits that you were investigating. I was window dressing, along for the money. The good life the money bought. And the thrill of being the mob's favorite hit duo. It was a rush knowing that every cop in Chicago was trying to lasso us."

"If I ever dreamed that Bill Sargent was one of them, it would have been a rush plus."

"You must admit we were good. Never a clue left behind for anyone to pick up our scent. I loved posing as an Irish hussy sending out those false signals as to the identity of the killers. My idea and contribution to the job."

"No cop ever thought to track us down for questioning. We were disappointed. Except you. You picked up on their goof up. Only you were smart enough to know that our charade was the link to all five hits."

"That's why I want you, Bill. Tully has worn out his welcome with me."

"Time is running short. Tully will find them and take them out. Today or tomorrow, and you too."

"Now let's get down to the heart of my proposition. I have a plan. I'm gonna hit Tully and want you to partner up with me. With Tully out of the way, we can do great things together. We hit the Balvianos ourselves and collect the million bucks from Masucci. He doesn't have to know that Tully cashed in his chips. All he cares about is a dead witness for the prosecution."

"By the time anyone figures it out, we'll be on an island somewhere in the Bahamas. I have two million bucks in a bank in the Caymans, and with the million from the Balviano hit we can lead the good life the rest of our lives."

"It's that simple, Bill. Masucci stays out of the joint. I get rid of Tully and get the man I really want. This is as good as it gets. Don't you agree?"

"Slow it down, lady. You're speaking so fast I can barely follow."

"I know. It's such an exciting prospect that I want to get it all out before you have a chance to say no."

"Do you really think I'd say yes?"

"Why not? What are you going to do with that small cop's pension? Just drink and fish and spend a drab rest of your life with whomever she is back in Chicago.?"

"Think of it. With me you'll be king, and I'll be your ever faithful queen. You'll still be able to drink and fish, but this time in style with a bank account that has lots of zeros. You'll bask in the hot sun with a cool drink in your hand. Not to mention a warm body in bed."

"So just say yes, Billy boy, and I'll bid farewell to Tully. You don't have to move a finger. Just tell me where the Bachs are and I can bid them farewell as well."

"Ah ha. Finally got to the point, love, although it was the roundabout way. You want me to finger the Bach's hideout so you and Tully can knock them off. Maybe take a shot at me, too."

"Real slick. Real slick. I should have seen it coming."

"Wrong Bill. Not Tully and me. You and me."

"Sure. You think you have me figured out. Your body, your money are lures that I can't resist. I'm not the dumb flatfoot you'd like to believe I am. It's not smart to think that."

"My instincts told me that you two were the two. It took me awhile to be sure. It's taken me a little longer to understand where you were coming from in this "proposition."

"Clever. A very clever ploy that I'm sure you master-minded."

"You fake Tully's death. Hit the Balvianos and then take me out. Tully miraculously comes to life. You collect the million dead presidents from Masucci and make your way to that island paradise before the Balvianos are in the ground. And everyone lives happily ever after."

"I love it. You and Tully know how to play games better than anyone. You've had lots of practice with your wild Irish charade."

"But I'm awake now, fully awake with my eyes wide open."

"You don't understand me at all. You don't know that I lost my way when Mary died. Found solace in a bottle. And even though retirement was all I could think, I was still a cop. A cop that never lost his integrity. Nobody can take that away from me. Certainly not you."

"Taking you down will be worth all those hours, days and years tracking you down. Worth more than a million bucks. And certainly worth more than a romp in the sack with you."

"The Balvianos will stay where they are for now. I don't care how much money passes around to his snitches. Nobody, not the Feds, not anyone in the Fire Department, not the Sheriff or any of his deputies know where they are. They'll stay put'til the Feds get them back to Chicago and Balviano testifies against your boss. And you go back with him. Under lock and key."

"It'll be a red letter day for me when Masucci takes his last breath of air on the outside. A wonderful day, when he is led inside the gates of a Federal prison for the rest of his miserable life."

"And if for some reason you and Tully don't get the needle for all the killing, you'll be following right behind him."

"The party's over, Mrs. Sullivan. No more thrills. No more adrenalin rushes. No more good life. NO way to spend your millions."

"The next time you see me I'll be putting bracelets on your bloody hands."

"You disappoint, Detective. I felt we had something going. Really did. But you're right, I did read you wrong. Now since you've turned your back on my proposition, I take back that smart cop label I placed on you. You are a dumb cop whose flat feet went to your brain."

"Oh well that's life in the fast lane."

"However, hold on to those cuffs, because we'll be out of here in minutes and now you'll have to find us."

"Don't delude yourself, Detective. We'll find the Balvianos and hit them hard. And you, too. Hopefully."

"If you live, enjoy your retirement."

"Don't get carried away with your bravado, Elaine. You can't go anywhere without lots of eyes following your every move. There's no way out."

"Once the Balvianos leave for Chicago, I'm coming for both of you. Now I'm going back to sleep and suggest you do likewise. Sleep tight tonight. And I hope Tully heard every word."

"Oh I almost forgot. Thanks for your proposition offer, it was very interesting."

"Detective Sargent? This is Linda Diner."

"Hello Linda. How are the kids?"

"They're fine, but I want..."

"How come you're calling me at 6:30 in the morning?

"I'm worried about Harry, Bill. He said he had an assignment in Naples, Florida to meet with you. Something about wrapping up a cold case. Whatever that means?"

"I haven't heard from him in two days, have you? Have you seen him or know where he is?"

"How did you get my number, Linda?"

"Harry gave it to me before he left. I'm worried sick. He never goes a few hours without calling."

"Harry did call me, Linda. We were supposed to meet, but he never showed. Maybe when I told him the cold case was ice cold he decided to go home."

"Harry didn't come home. It's two days now, that's why I'm calling you."

"Oh, I wouldn't worry Linda, Harry probably visited some old friends living in Naples and forgot what day it was."

"What old friends? He doesn't know anyone in Naples, much less Florida. He's never been out of Chicago."

"You know Harry, he is really forgetful. Maybe he's working on a different lead that the Captain gave him. Maybe tied him up for a while. Stay calm. I'm sure he'll call or walk in the door shortly. If he contacts me, I'll make sure he calls you first thing."

"Sorry I can't help, but I gotta go Linda."

An hour later the phone rang again. He picked up and without waiting to hear a voice he yelled out, "Elaine it's still too early and the answer is still no."

"Detective, is that you? It's Sheriff Hunter."

"Sorry about that Sheriff. What's up?"

"The Sullivans were shot early this morning."

"What? Shot? By whom?"

"Don't know. As far as we can determine it was about 4AM."

"Are they able to identify the shooter?

"Hardly, Detective. They're dead."

"Dead? Oh my god. I just spoke to Elaine Sullivan a few hours ago. Masucci's goons must have gotten to them. He didn't like the delay, He had them taken down and then it would be Balviano's turn. Gotta get to him before they do."

"Nobody knows where you've got them."

"For now. Gotta run Sheriff."

"Wait up Bill, where do you have them? Let me send some of my deputies to help out."

"Nah. No time for that. Will call you."

Sargent jumped in his car and sped off to the motel. Everything was quiet in the lobby. The desk clerk was drinking coffee and reading the morning paper. He looked up and came face-to-face with an out-of-breath, very agitated Detective Sargent.

"Good morning, sir, can I help you? Do you have a reservation?"

"I'm Detective Sargent," showing his badge," was there any trouble early this morning?"

"Trouble? What kind of trouble?"

"Any strangers hanging around or checking in?"

"No strangers, nobody checking in. You're the first person here, except for the newspaper delivery guy."

"Did the couple in 210 check out?"

"Just started my shift at 7AM and nobody's checked out since I'm on."

"What about earlier?"

"Could be. Not usual, but could be. Let me check 210."

"Yes sir, here it is. The Bachs in 210 checked out."

"What time?"

"Three AM."

"Isn't that an odd time to check out?"

"Very odd, but in places near highways and airports it's quite possible. Wait a minute, the nite clerk left a note saying 210 received a long distance call about 2:30, something about an emergency. Checked out shortly after. They paid in cash, even though we had a credit card on file. Told the desk clerk not to mention anything to anyone."

Sargent raced up the stairs and found the door to 210 slightly ajar. He pulled his gun and slowly entered. The Balvianos were gone. Only half eaten containers of Chinese food were strewn around the room. Then he noticed a handwritten note on the bed addressed to him.

Sargent/Cop

Sorry we had to leave without calling you. Made a pact with the devil to get rid of the devils. Masucci made an offer we couldn't refuse. He agreed to pay us a million big ones to hit the Sullivans. Good thing I had my piece with me. So we won't be testifying against him. It's a done deal. He gave me his word of honor that they won't come after us. Give the Feds our best. We don't need the Witness Protection Program anymore, cause we ain't testifying to anything. By the time you read this the micks will be dead. Don't try and find us. We're out of paradise on our way to a a Shangri-la somewhere with a million clams in our pocket. Thanks for caring about us. Carmen thinks you're an ok guy for a cop.

Sebastian/Salvatore

Sargent sat on the bed somewhat in disbelief at the turn of events. He took out a cigar and lit up for the first time in years. With the first puff he let out a hearty laugh. Cops and robbers. How do you figure, he thought to himself? The hitters get hit. The big bucks go to the hittee. The crime world turned upside down. He picked up the phone and called Sheriff Hunter.

"Sargent, is everything ok with the Bachs?"

"Peachy, Sheriff. They're the ones that killed the Sullivans and are on the lam. Masucci paid them the million bucks to make the hit and not to testify. How about them apples?"

"That's the whole fruit stand, Detective."

"Should I put an APB out for the Bachs?"

"Nah. Let them be. It's too good an ending to an unbelievable story. No, let them be."

"What about the FBI?"

"Who cares?"

"What'll I do with the Sulllvan bodies?"

"Ship them to Masucci in Chicago, C.O.D. Include a note telling him he got his money's worth: a free, get-out-of-jail card."

When Sargent returned to the Inn, three agents were parked out in front of his room. Pacing up and down the hall.

"Glad you got back, Detective," said the lead agent.

"Great to see you guys too."

"You're under arrest for obstruction of justice, facilitating and tampering with someone on the Witness Protection Program, kidnapping that person, aiding and abetting in the murder of two citizens, and allowing the killer to escape."

"You left out one charge, Mr. G-Man. What about threatening a Federal officer with bodily harm?"

"This is no laughing matter, Sargent. You are going to jail."

"Nah, I don't think so. The U.S. Attorney will throw out every charge when he hears what I have to say. It's all down on paper for him. So my good man, please get out of my way, I hear my phone ringing."

"Sargent this is the Captain. What the hell is going down down there? I want a report immediately."

"Nothing much Captain. Oh just one small thing. The cold case file is now officially closed. Tully and Elaine Sullivan were the two hit men that killed those five people."

"Are you bringing them in you excuse for a cop?"

"Can't do, Captain. You see Texas justice was done when they were shot dead themselves."

"You or other cops?"

"It may be hard to believe, sir, but the Witness for the Prosecution, Mr. Salvatore Balviano, was the culprit. I want you to know that I had them all wrapped up, when he pulled the trigger."

"The real kicker Captain, sir is that the Balvianos got the million bucks from Masucci to hit the Sullivans instead of vice versa. I guess he felt it was a small price to guarantee no witness testimony, no jail time. How about them apples?"

"When are you bringing Balviano back? He may not have to testify, but he can't get away with murder."

"I couldn't agree with you more, but he ain't coming back. Not with me anyhow."

"What did you screw up now, Sarge?"

"Nothing I did. Balviano flew the coop, destination unknown. He exchanged the Witness Protection Program for the Masucci Survival program."

"Nevertheless, that's not my concern, sir. The case against the duo that committed five hits is now officially closed. My last job is at last done. Put in my papers."

"By the way, one of your dirty cops is dead, too. Diner ate his own gun. Check your squad room for some others that are probably on Masucci's Xmas list."

"I know you'll probably shed tears for what else I'm about to tell you, so get a hankie ready. The Feds have arrested me. It's a long story. Ask my PBA lawyer to bone up on how to get around interfering with someone on The Federal Witness Protection Program."

"Also notify the U.S. Attorney that I've got a confession note from the protected witness himself that will prove that Masucci is guilty of bribing a Federal witness and facilitating a double murder. Not to mention ordering the five hits he paid the

Sullivans to commit. That should put him away forever and a day. Witness or no witness."

"Are you still with me, Captain sir? When you close the cold case file, I suggest opening a new one on Salvatore Balviano. He murdered two murderers. Doesn't call for mercy, though. Use your supreme command influence to assign another detective you dislike to track him down. It might take a few years, but knowing you it'll give you lots of time to get to hate him."

"See you in Chicago. Thanks for the use of an unlimited expense account which I exceeded by quite a bit."

"Oh, and last but not least, turn in my papers, you excuse for a Captain."

Sargent hung up without waiting for an answer.

ABOUT THE AUTHOR

L.C. Goldman (Lou to friends and family) was a star athlete in high school and college and an advertising agency executive for over forty years supervising major consumer names such as: Seagram, The Concorde (SST), Perrier Jouet Champagne, Ralph Lauren, Polo and Chaps Colognes, Yves St. Laurent and Armitron Watches.

He follows up his first novel, "AND THE PEACE CAME TUMBLING DOWN", a story as topical as today's headlines about the Middle East peace process, with a murder mystery set in Pelican Bay in Naples, Florida.

L.C. is retired and living in Pelican Bay writing novels, playing golf and involved in many community activities.